BY CHARLES BUKOWSKI

The Days Run Away Like Wild Horses Over the Hills (1969)

Post Office (1971)

Mockingbird Wish Me Luck (1972)

South of No North (1973)

Burning in Water, Drowning in Flame: Selected Poems 1955–1973 (1974)

Factotum (1975)

Love Is a Dog from Hell: Poems 1974–1977 (1977)

Women (1978)

You Kissed Lilly (1978)

Play the piano drunk Like a percussion Instrument Until the fingers begin to bleed a bit (1979)

Shakespeare Never Did This (1979)

Dangling in the Tournefortia (1981)

Ham on Rye (1982)

Bring Me Your Love (1983)

Hot Water Music (1983)

There's No Business (1984)

War All the Time: Poems 1981–1984 (1984)

You Get So Alone At Times That It Just Makes Sense (1986)

The Movie: "Barfly" (1987)

The Roominghouse Madrigals: Early Selected Poems 1946–1966 (1988)

Hollywood (1989)

Septuagenarian Stew: Stories & Poems (1990)

The Last Night of the Earth Poems (1992)

Screams from the Balcony: Selected Letters 1960–1970 (Volume 1) (1993)

Pulp (1994)

Living on Luck: Selected Letters 1960s–1970s (Volume 2) (1995)

Betting on the Muse: Poems & Stories (1996)

Bone Palace Ballet: New Poems (1997)

The Captain Is Out to Lunch and the Sailors Have Taken Over the Ship (1998)

Reach for the Sun: Selected Letters 1978–1994 (Volume 3) (1999)

What Matters Most Is How Well You Walk Through the Fire: New Poems (1999)

Open All Night: New Poems (2000)

Beerspit Night and Cursing: The Correspondence of Charles Bukowski & Sheri Martinelli (2001)

The Night Torn Mad with Footsteps: New Poems (2001)

Sifting Through the Madness for the Word, the Line, the Way: New Poems (2002)

CHARLES BUKOWSKI

Burning in Water Drowning in Flame

ecco

An Imprint of HarperCollins Publishers

BURNING IN WATER, DROWNING IN FLAME. Copyright © 1963, 1964, 1965, 1966, 1967, 1968, 1974 by Charles Bukowski. All rights reserved. Printed in the United States of America. No part of this book may be used or reproduced in any manner whatsoever without written permission except in the case of brief quotations embodied in critical articles and reviews. For information address HarperCollins Publishers Inc., 10 East 53rd Street, New York, NY 10022.

HarperCollins books may be purchased for educational, business, or sales promotional use. For information please write: Special Markets Department, HarperCollins Publishers Inc., 10 East 53rd Street, New York, NY 10022.

The poems in the first three sections of this book were originally published in three volumes now long out of print: *It Catches My Heart in Its Hands* (Loujon Press, 1968), *Crucifix in a Deathhand* (Loujon Press in collaboration with Lyle Stuart, Inc., 1965), and *At Terror Street and Agony Way* (Black Sparrow Press, 1968). The author would like to give acknowledgment to the publishers of these volumes, Jon and Louise Webb, Lyle Stuart, and John Martin.

The author would like to thank the National Endowment for the Arts for a grant on which the poems in the final section of this book was written.

First Ecco edition 2003.

Library of Congress Cataloging-in-Publication Data

ISBN 0-87685-191-X (PAPER EDITION)
ISBN 0-87685-192-8 (TRADE CLOTH EDITION)

11 12 13 ❖RRD 20 19

for Steve Richmond

AUTHOR'S INTRODUCTION

The poems in the first three sections of this book are from the years 1955-1968 and the poems in the last section are the new work of 1972-1973. The reader might wonder what happened to the years 1969-1971, since the author once did vanish (literally) from 1944 to 1954. But not this time. *The Days Run Away Like Wild Horses Over The Hills* (Black Sparrow Press, 1969) contains the poems from late 1968 and most of 1969, plus selections from five early chapbooks not covered by the first three sections of this book. *Mockingbird Wish Me Luck* (Black Sparrow Press, 1972) prints poems written from late 1969 to early 1972. So, for my critics, readers, friends, enemies, ex-lovers and new lovers, the present volume along with *Days* and *Mockingbird* contain what I like to consider my best work written over the past nineteen years.

Each of these sections brings back special memories. For *It Catches My Heart In Its Hands* I was required to make a trip to New Orleans. The editor first had to check me out to see if I was a decent human being. Catching the train at the Union Station just below the Terminal Annex of the Post Office where I worked for Uncle Sam, I sat in the bar car and drank scotch and water and sped toward New Orleans to be judged and measured by an ex-con who owned an ancient printing press. Jon Webb believed that most writers (and he'd met some good ones including Sherwood Anderson, Faulkner, Hemingway) were detestable human beings when they were away from their typewriters. I arrived, they met me, Jon and his wife, Louise, we drank and talked for two weeks, then Jon Webb said, "You're a bastard, Bukowski, but I'm going to publish you anyhow." I left town. But that wasn't all. Soon they were both in Los Angeles with their two dogs in a green hotel just off skid row. Re-check. Drink and talk. I was still a bastard. Goodbye. Much leaving and waving through train windows. Louise cried through the glass. *It Catches* was published . . .

The bulk of the poems in *Crucifix In A Deathhand* were written during one very hot, lyrical month in New Orleans in the year 1965. I'd walk down the street and I'd stagger, sober I'd stagger, hear churchbells, wounded dogs, wounded me, all that. I had gone into a slump or a blackout after the publication of *It Catches*, and Jon and Louise had brought me back down to New Orleans. I lived right around the corner from them with a fat, kind woman whose ex-husband (who'd died) had come very close to being welterweight or middleweight champion of the world, I forget which. Each night I went over to Jon and Louise's and we drank until early morning at a small table in the kitchen with the roaches running up and down the wall in front of us (they particularly liked to circle around an unshaded lightbulb sticking out of the wall) as we drank and talked.

I would go back to my place and awaken about 10:30 a.m., quite sick. I'd dress and walk over to Jon's place. The press was below street level and I'd peek down at him before I knocked. I could see him through the window, calm, cool, hardly hungover at all, humming, and feeding pages of *Crucifix* into the press.

"Got any poems, Bukowski?" he'd ask as I walked in. (One had to be careful: feeding poems into a waiting press can easily dissolve into journalism.)

Jon would become downright unlaced if I didn't have a handful of poems. It wasn't as pleasant to be around that bastard then, and I'd find myself back in my room beating the typer. In the evening, if I brought him a little sheaf of poems, his mood would be better.

So I kept writing poems. We drank with the roaches, the place was small, and pages 5, 6, 7 and 8 were stacked in the bathtub, nobody could bathe, and pages 1, 2, 3 and 4 were in a large trunk, and soon there wasn't anyplace to put anything. There were 7-and-one-half foot stacks of pages everywhere. Very carefully we moved between them. The bathtub had been useful but the bed was in the way. So Jon built a little loft out of discarded lumber. Plus a stairway. And Jon and Louise slept up there on a mattress and the bed was given away. There was more floor space to stack the pages. "Bukowski, Bukowski everywhere! I am going crazy!" said Louise. The roaches circled and we drank and the press gulped my poems. A very strange time, and that was *Crucifix* . . .

I used to go to John Thomas' place and stay all night. We'd take pills and drink and talk. That is, John took the pills and I took the pills *and* drank, and we both talked. John was then in the habit of taping everything, whether it was good or bad, dull or interesting, worthless or useful. We would listen to our conversations the next day, and it *was* a worthwhile process, at least for me. I realized how oafish and overbearing and off-target I often was, at least when I was high. And sometimes when I wasn't.

At one time during these tapings John asked that I bring over some poems and read them. I did. And left the poems there and forgot about them. The poems were thrown out with the garbage. Months passed. One day Thomas phoned me. "Those poems, Bukowski, would make a good book." "What poems, John?" He said he had taken out the tape of my poems and had listened to it again. "I'd have to type them off the tape, it's just too much work," I said. "I'll type them up for you." I agreed, and soon I had the poems back in typescript form.

At this time a balding red-haired man with a high, scrubbed forehead, meticulous and kind, with a very faint, perpetual grin was coming by. He worked as the manager of an office furniture and supply company and was a collector of rare books. His name was John Martin. He had published some of my poems as broadsides. He wrote me out checks as I sat in my kitchen across from him, drinking beer and signing the broadsides. It was the beginning of the Black Sparrow Press, a house that was soon to begin publishing a large portion of America's avant-garde poetry, but neither of us knew it then.

I showed John Martin the poems Thomas had typed off the tape for me. I had checked his transcriptions, and he'd done a careful, accurate job. John Martin took the poems home with him and phoned me a couple of days later: "You have a book there and I'm going to publish it myself." And that's how some almost lost poems were found again and printed in book form and the Black Sparrow was flying. I called the book *At Terror Street And Agony Way.*

Looking at these poems written between 1955 and 1973 I like (for one reason or another) the last poems best. I am pleased with this. I have, of course, no idea what shape my future poems will take, or even if I will write any, because I have no idea how long I will go on living, but since I began writing poetry quite late in life, at the age of 35, I like to think they'll give me a few extra years now, at this end. Meanwhile, the poems that follow will have to do.

Charles Bukowski
January 30, 1974

Table of Contents

At Terror Street and Agony Way (Poems 1965-1968)

I

It Catches
My Heart
in
Its Hands

Poems 1955-1963

lay down
lay down and wait like
an animal

the tragedy of the leaves

I awakened to dryness and the ferns were dead,
the potted plants yellow as corn;
my woman was gone
and the empty bottles like bled corpses
surrounded me with their uselessness;
the sun was still good, though,
and my landlady's note cracked in fine and
undemanding yellowness; what was needed now
was a good comedian, ancient style, a jester
with jokes upon absurd pain; pain is absurd
because it exists, nothing more;
I shaved carefully with an old razor
the man who had once been young and
said to have genius; but
that's the tragedy of the leaves,
the dead ferns, the dead plants;
and I walked into a dark hall
where the landlady stood
execrating and final,
sending me to hell,
waving her fat, sweaty arms
and screaming
screaming for rent
because the world had failed us
both.

to the whore who took my poems

some say we should keep personal remorse from the
poem,
stay abstract, and there is some reason in this,
but jezus;
twelve poems gone and I don't keep carbons and you have
my
paintings too, my best ones; it's stifling:
are you trying to crush me out like the rest of them?
why didn't you take my money? they usually do
from the sleeping drunken pants sick in the corner.
next time take my left arm or a fifty
but not my poems:
I'm not Shakespeare
but sometime simply
there won't be any more, abstract or otherwise;
there'll always be money and whores and drunkards
down to the last bomb,
but as God said,
crossing his legs,
I see where I have made plenty of poets
but not so very much
poetry.

the state of world affairs
from a 3rd floor window

I am watching a girl dressed in a
light green sweater, blue shorts, long black stockings;
there is a necklace of some sort
but her breasts are small, poor thing,
and she watches her nails
as her dirty white dog sniffs the grass
in erratic circles;
a pigeon is there too, circling,
half dead with a tick of a brain
and I am upstairs in my underwear,
3 day beard, pouring a beer and waiting
for something literary or symphonic to happen;
but they keep circling, circling, and a thin old man
in his last winter rolls by pushed by a girl
in a catholic school dress;
somewhere there are the Alps, and ships
are now crossing the sea;
there are piles and piles of H- and A-bombs,
enough to blow up fifty worlds and Mars thrown in,
but they keep circling,
the girl shifts buttocks,
and the Hollywood Hills stand there, stand there
full of drunks and insane people and
much kissing in automobiles,
but it's no good: *che sera, sera:*
her dirty white dog simply will not shit,
and with a last look at her nails
she, with much whirling of buttocks
walks to her downstairs court
trailed by her constipated dog (simply not worried),
leaving me looking at a most unsymphonic pigeon.
well, from the looks of things, relax:
the bombs will never go off.

for marilyn m.

slipping keenly into bright ashes,
target of vanilla tears
your sure body lit candles for men
on dark nights,
and now your night is darker
than the candle's reach
and we will forget you, somewhat,
and it is not kind
but real bodies are nearer
and as the worms pant for your bones,
I would so like to tell you
that this happens to bears and elephants
to tyrants and heroes and ants
and frogs,
still, you brought us something,
some type of small victory,
and for this I say: good
and let us grieve no more;
like a flower dried and thrown away,
we forget, we remember,
we wait. child, child, child,
I raise my drink a full minute
and smile.

the life of borodin

the next time you listen to Borodin
remember he was just a chemist
who wrote music to relax;
his house was jammed with peor e:
students, artists, drunkards, bur s,
and he never knew how to say: no.
the next time you listen to Borodin
remember his wife used his compositions
to line the cat boxes with
or to cover jars of sour milk;
she had asthma and insomnia
and fed him soft-boiled eggs
and when he wanted to cover his head
to shut out the sounds of the house
she only allowed him to use the sheet;
besides there was usually somebody
in his bed
(they slept separately when they slept
at all)
and since all the chairs
were usually taken
he often slept on the stairway
wrapped in an old shawl;
she told him when to cut his nails,
not to sing or whistle
or put too much lemon in his tea
or press it with a spoon;
Symphony #2, in B Minor
Prince Igor
On the Steppes of Central Asia
he could sleep only by putting a piece
of dark cloth over his eyes;
in 1887 he attended a dance
at the Medical Academy
dressed in a merrymaking national costume;
at last he seemed exceptionally gay
and when he fell to the floor,
they thought he was clowning.
the next time you listen to Borodin,
remember . . .

no charge

this babe in the grandstand
with dyed red hair
kept leaning her breasts against me
and talking about Gardena
poker parlors
but I blew smoke into
her face
and told her about a Van Gogh
exhibition
I'd seen up on the hill
and that night
when I took her home
she said
Big Red was the best horse
she'd ever seen —
until I stripped down. Though I
think on the Van Gogh thing
they charged
50 cents.

a literary romance

I met her somehow through correspondence or poetry or magazines
and she began sending me very sexy poems about rape and lust,
and this being mixed in with a minor intellectualism
confused me somewhat and I got in my car and drove North
through the mountains and valleys and freeways
without sleep, coming off a drunk, just divorced,
jobless, aging, tired, wanting mostly to sleep
for five or ten years, I finally found the motel
in a small sunny town by a dirt road,
and I sat there smoking a cigarette
thinking, you must really be insane,
and then I got out an hour late
to meet my date; she was pretty damned old,
almost as old as I, not very sexy
and she gave me a very hard raw apple
which I chewed on with my remaining teeth;
she was dying of some unnamed disease
something like asthma, and she said,
I want to tell you a secret, and I said,
I know: you are a virgin, 35 years old.
and she got out a notebook, ten or twelve poems:
a life's work and I had to read them
and I tried to be kind
but they were very bad.
and I took her somewhere, the boxing matches,
and she coughed in the smoke
and kept looking around and around
at all the people
and then at the fighters
clenching her hands.
you never get excited, do you? she asked.
but I got pretty excited in the hills that night,
and met her three or four more times
helped her with some of her poems
and she rammed her tongue halfway down my throat
but when I left her
she was still a virgin
and a very bad poetess.
I think that when a woman has kept her legs closed

21

for 35 years
it's too late
either for love
or for
poetry.

the twins

he hinted at times that I was a bastard and I told him to listen
to Brahms, and I told him to learn to paint and drink and not be
dominated by women and dollars
but he screamed at me, For Christ's Sake remember your mother,
remember your country,
you'll kill us all! . . .

I move through my father's house (on which he owed $8,000 after 20
years on the same job) and look at his dead shoes
the way his feet curled the leather, as if he was angrily planting roses,
and he was, and I look at his dead cigarette, his last cigarette
and the last bed he slept in that night, and I feel I should remake it
but I can't, for a father is always your master even when he's gone;
I guess these things have happened time and again but I can't help
thinking

> to die on a kitchen floor at 7 o'clock in the morning
> while other people are frying eggs
> is not so rough
> unless it happens to you.

I go outside and pick an orange and peel back the bright skin;
things are still living: the grass is growing quite well,
the sun sends down its rays circled by a Russian satellite,
a dog barks senselessly somewhere, the neighbors peek behind blinds.
I am a stranger here, and have been (I suppose) somewhat the rogue,
and I have no doubt he painted me quite well (the old boy and I
fought like mountain lions) and they say he left it all to some woman
in Duarte but I don't give a damn — she can have it: he was my old
man

> and he died.

inside, I try on a light blue suit
much better than anything I have ever worn
and I flap the arms like a scarecrow in the wind
but it's no good:

I can't keep him alive
no matter how much we hated each other.

we looked exactly alike, we could have been twins
the old man and I: that's what they
said. he had his bulbs on the screen
ready for planting
while I was lying with a whore from 3rd street.

very well. grant us this moment: standing before a mirror
in my dead father's suit
waiting also
to die.

the day it rained
at the los angeles
county museum

the jew bent over and
                    died. 99 machine guns
were shipped to France. somebody won the 3rd race
while I inspected
                    the propeller of an old monoplane
a man came by with a patch over his eye. it began to
rain. it rained and it rained and the ambulances ran
together
in the streets, and although
everything was properly dull
I enjoyed the moment
like the time in New Orleans
living on candy bars
and watching the pigeons
in a back alley with a French name
as behind me the river became
a gulf
and the clouds moved sickly through
a sky that had died
about the time Caesar was knifed,
and I promised myself then
that someday I'd remember it
as it was.

a man came by and coughed.
think it'll stop raining? he said.
I didn't answer. I touched the
old propeller and listened to the
ants on the roof rushing over
the edge of the world. go away, I said,
go away or I'll call
the guard.

2 p.m. beer

nothing matters
but flopping on a mattress
with cheap dreams and a beer
as the leaves die and the horses die
and the landladies stare in the halls;
brisk the music of pulled shades,
a last man's cave
in an eternity of swarm
and explosion;
nothing but the dripping sink,
the empty bottle,
euphoria,
youth fenced in,
stabbed and shaven,
taught words
propped up
to die.

hooray say the roses

hooray say the roses, today is blamesday
and we are red as blood.

hooray say the roses, today is Wednesday
and we bloom where soldiers fell,
and lovers too,
and the snake ate the word.

hooray say the roses, darkness comes
all at once, like lights gone out,
the sun leaves dark continents
and rows of stone.

hooray say the roses, cannons and spires,
birds, bees, bombers, today is Friday
the hand holding a medal out the window,
a moth going by, half a mile an hour,
hooray hooray
hooray say the roses
we wave empires on our stems,
the sun moves the mouth:
hooray hooray hooray
and that is why you like us.

the sunday artist

I have been painting these last two Sundays;
it's not much, you're correct,
but in this tournament great dreams break:
history removes her dress and becomes a harlot,
and I have awakened in the morning
to see eagles flapping their wings like shades;
I have met Montaigne and Phidias
in the flames of my wastebasket,
I have met barbarians on the streets
their heads rocking with rodents;
I have seen wicked infants in blue tubs
wanting stems as beautiful as flowers,
and I have seen the barfly sick
over his last dead penny;
I have heard Domenico Theotocopoulos
on nights of frost, cough in his grave;
and God, no taller than a landlady,
hair dyed red, has asked me the time;
I have seen grey grass of lovers in my mirror
while lighting a cigarette to a maniac's applause;
Cadillacs have crawled my walls like roaches,
goldfish whirl my bowl, hand-tamed tigers;
yes, I have been painting these Sundays —
the grey mill, the new rebel; it's terrible really:
I must ram my fist through cleanser and chlorine,
through Andernach and apples and acid,
but, then, I really should tell you that I have a
woman around mixing waffle flour and singing,
and the paint sticks to my plan like candy.

old poet

I would, of course, prefer to be with the fox in the ferns
instead of with a photograph of an old Spad in my pocket
to the sound of the anvil chorus and legs legs legs
girls kicking high, showing everything but the pisser,
but I might as well be dead right now

      everywhere the ill wind blows
      and Keats is dead
      and I am dying too.

for there is nothing as crappy dissolute
as an old poet gone sour
in body and mind
and luck, the horses running nothing but out,
the Vegas dice cancer to the thin green wallet,
Shostakovich heard too often
and cans of beer sucked through a straw,
with mouth and mind broken in
young men's alleys.
in the hot noon window
I swing and miss a razzing fly,
and ho, I fall heavy as thunder
but downstairs they'll understand:
he's either drunk or dying,
an old poet nodding vaguely in halls,
cracking his stick across the backs
of innocent dogs
and spitting out
what's left of his sun.
the mailman has some little thing for him
which he takes to his room
and opens like a rose,
only to scream loudly and vainly,
and his coffin is filled
with notes from hell.
but in the morning you'll see him
packing off little envelopes,
still worried about
rent
     cigarettes
          wine

                    women
                            horses,
still worried about
Eric Coates, Beethoven's 3rd and
something Chicago has held for three months
and his paper bag of wine
and Pall Malls.
42 in August, 42,
the rats walking his brain
eating up the thoughts before they
can make the keys.
old poets are as bad as old queers:
there's something quite unacceptable:
the editors wish to thank you for
submitting but
regret . . .
down
        down
                down
                        the dark hall
into a womanless hall
to peel a last egg
and sit down to the keys:
click click a click,
over the television sounds
over the sounds of springs,
click clack a clack:
another old poet
going off.

the race

it is like this
when you slip down,
done like a wound-up victrola
(you remember those?)
and you go downtown
and watch the boys punch
but the big blondes sit with
someone else
and you've aged like a punk in a movie:
cigar in skull, fat gut,
but only no money,
no wiseness of way, no worldliness,
but as usual
most of the fights are bad,
and afterwards
back in the parking lot
you sit and watch them go,
light the last cigar,
and then start the old car,
old car, not so young man
going down the street
stopped by a red light
as if time were no problem,
and they come up to you:
a car full of young,
laughing,
and you watch them go
until
somebody behind you honks
and you are shaken back
into what is left
of your life.
pitiful, self-pity,
and your foot is to the floor
and you catch the young ones,
you pass the young ones
and holding the wheel like all love gone
you race to the beach
with them
brandishing your cigar and your steel,
laughing,

you will take them to the ocean
to the last mermaid,
seaweed and shark, merry whale,
end of flesh and hour and horror,
and finally they stop
and you go on
toward your ocean,
the cigar biting your lips
the way love used to.

vegas

there was a frozen tree that I wanted to paint
but the shells came down
and in Vegas looking across at a green sunshade
at 3:30 in the morning,
I died without nails, without a copy of the *Atlantic Monthly*,
the windows screamed like doves moaning the bombing of Milan
and I went out to live with the rats
but the lights were too bright
and I thought maybe I'd better go back and sit in a
poetry class:

      a marvelous description of a gazelle
      is hell;
      the cross sits like a fly on my window,
      my mother's breath stirs small leaves
      in my mind;

and I hitch-hiked back to L.A. through hangover clouds
and I pulled a letter from my pocket and read it
and the truckdriver said, what's that?
and I said, there's some gal up North who used to
sleep with Pound, she's trying to tell me that H.D.
was our greatest scribe; well, Hilda gave us a few pink
Grecian gods in with the chinaware, but after reading her
I still have 140 icicles hanging from my bones.

I'm not going all the way to L.A., the truckdriver said.

it's all right, I said, the calla lilies nod to our minds
and someday we'll all go home
together.

in fact, he said, this is as far
as we go.
so I let him have it; old withered whore of time
your breasts taste the sour cream of dreaming . . .
he let me out
in the middle of the desert;

to die is to die is to die,

old phonographs in cellars,
joe di maggio,
magazines in with the onions . . .

an old Ford picked me up
45 minutes later
and, this time,
I kept my mouth
shut.

the house

they are building a house
half a block down
and I sit up here
with the shades down
listening to the sounds,
the hammers pounding in nails,
thack thack thack thack,
and then I hear birds, and
thack thack thack
and I go to bed,
I pull the covers to my throat;
they have been building this house
for a month, and soon it will have
its people . . . sleeping, eating,
loving, moving around,
but somehow
now
it is not right,
there seems a madness,
men walk on its top with nails in their mouths
and I read about Castro and Cuba,
and at night I walk by
and the ribs of house show
and inside I can see cats walking
the way cats walk,
and then a boy rides by on a bicycle,
and still the house is not done
and in the morning the men
will be back
walking around on the house
with their hammers,
and it seems people should not build houses
anymore,
it seems people should stop working
and sit in small rooms
on second floors
under electric lights without shades;
it seems there is a lot to forget
and a lot not to do
and in drugstores, markets, bars,
the people are tired, they do not want

to move, and I stand there at night
and look through this house and the
house does not **want** to be built;
through its sides I can see the purple hills
and the first lights of evening,
and it is cold
and I button my coat
and I stand there looking through the house
and the cats stop and look at me
until I am embarrassed
and move North up the sidewalk
where I will buy
cigarettes and beer
and return to my room.

side of the sun

the bulls are grand as the side of the sun
and although they kill them for the stale crowds,
it is the bull that burns the fire,
and although there are cowardly bulls as
there are cowardly matadors and cowardly men,
generally the bull stands pure
and dies pure
untouched by symbols or cliques or false loves,
and when they drag him out
nothing has died
something has passed
and the eventual stench
is the world.

the talkers

the boy walks with his muddy feet across my
soul
talking about recitals, virtuosi, conductors,
the lesser known novels of Dostoevsky;
talking about how he corrected a waitress,
a hasher who didn't know that French dressing
was composed of *so and so;*
he gabbles about the Arts until
I hate the Arts,
and there is nothing cleaner
than getting back to a bar or
back to the track and watching them run,
watching things go without this
clamor and chatter,
talk, talk, talk,
the small mouth going, the eyes blinking,
a boy, a child, sick with the Arts,
grabbing at it like the skirt of a mother,
and I wonder how many tens of thousands
there are like him across the land
on rainy nights
on sunny mornings
on evenings meant for peace
in concert halls
in cafes
at poetry recitals
talking, soiling, arguing.

it's like a pig going to bed
with a good woman
and you don't want
the woman any more.

a pleasant afternoon in bed

red summers and black satin
charcoal and blood
ringing the sheets
while snails are stepped on
and moths go batty
trying to put on the eyes
of lightbulbs in
artificial cities;
I light her a cigarette
and she blows up a plasma
of relaxation
to prove we've both been
good lovers —
white on black, and in black;
and her toes strike dark
intersections
in my beefy sheets
she says, that elevator boy . . .
y'know him?
I say yes.
a bastard . . . beats his wife.
I put my hand
flat to the surface
where the curve goes down.
damn for an OLD man,
you sure likes to play!
I reach over and pick up
the bottle, suck it down
flat on my back,
the suds like soap
gagging me with gulp-dull
sounds, and she's listening,
eyes rolling
like newsreel cameras,
and suddenly I have got to laugh,
I spiral out a whale-stream
of foam and liquid
majestic against the wallpaper
not knowing why,
and she laughs
looking down at my flat madness,

she laughs
holding her cigarette
high in the air
with one arm
smoke sifting off
ignored
and we are in bed together
laughing
and we don't care
about anything
and it is very
very funny.

the priest and the matador

in the slow Mexican air I watched the bull die
and they cut off his ear, and his great head held
no more terror than a rock.

driving back the next day we stopped at the Mission
and watched the golden red and blue flowers pulling
like tigers in the wind.

set this to metric: the bull, and the fort of Christ:
the matador on his knees, the dead bull his baby;
and the priest staring from the window
like a caged bear.

you may argue in the market place and pull at your
doubts with silken strings: I will only tell you
this: I have lived in both their temples,
believing all and nothing — perhaps, now, they will
die in mine.

love & fame & death

it sits outside my window now
like an old woman going to market;
it sits and watches me,
it sweats nervously
through wire and fog and dog-bark
until suddenly
I slam the screen with a newspaper
like slapping at a fly
and you could hear the scream
over this plain city,
and then it left.

the way to end a poem
like this
is to become suddenly
quiet.

my father

he carried a piece of
carbon, a blade and a whip
and at night he
feared his head
and covered it with blankets
until one morning in Los Angeles
it snowed
and I saw the snow
and I knew that my father
could control nothing,
and when
I got somewhat larger
and took my first boxcar
out, I sat there in
the lime
the burning lime
of having nothing
moving into the desert
for the first time
I sang.

the bird

red-eyed and dizzy as I
the bird came flying
all the way from Egypt
at 5 o'clock in the morning,
and Maria almost stumbled on her spikes:
what was it, a rocket?
and we went upstairs.
I poured two glasses of port
and we sat there as the money-grubbers
were belled out of their miserable nests
and Maria went in and watered
the bowl
and I sat there rubbing my three-day beard
thinking about the crazy bird
and it came out like this:
all that really mattered was
going someplace
the faster the better
because it left less waiting
to die. Maria came out
and peeled back the covers
and I tore off my greasy clothes
and crawled beneath the sweaty sheets,
closing my eyes to the sound and the sunlight,
and I heard her drop her spiked feet
and her frozen toes walked the backs of my calves
and I named the bird
Mr. America
and then quickly I went to sleep.

the singular self

there are these small cliffs
above the sea
and it is night, late night;
I have been unable to sleep,
and with my car above me
like a steel mother
I crawl down the cliffs,
breaking bits of rock
and being scratched by witless
and scrabby seaplants,
I make my way down
clumsy, misplaced,
an oddity on the shore,
and all around me are the lovers,
the two-headed beasts
turning to stare
at the madness
of a singular self;
shamed, I move on through them
to climb a row of wet boulders that
break the sea-stroke
into sheaths of white;
the moonlight is wet
on the bald stone
and now that I'm there
I don't want to be there
the sea stinks
and makes flushing sounds
like a toilet
it is a bad place to die;
any place is a bad place to die,
but better a yellow room
with known walls and dusty
lampshades; so . . .
still stupidly off-course
like a jackal in a land of lions,
I make my way back through
them, through their blankets
and fires and kisses and sandy thumpings,
back up the cliff I climb

worse off, kicking clods,
and there the black sky, the black sea
behind me
lost in the game,
and I have left my shoes down there
with them   2 empty shoes,
and in the car
I start the engine,
headlights on I back away,
swing left drive East,
climb up the land and out,
bare feet on worn ribbed rubber
out of there
looking for
another place.

a 340 dollar horse and a hundred dollar whore

don't ever get the idea I am a poet; you can see me
at the racetrack any day half drunk
betting quarters, sidewheelers and straight thoroughs,
but let me tell you, there are some women there
who go where the money goes, and sometimes when you
look at these whores these onehundreddollar whores
you wonder sometimes if nature isn't playing a joke
dealing out so much breast and ass and the way
it's all hung together, you look and you look and
you look and you can't believe it; there are ordinary women
and then there is something else that wants to make you
tear up paintings and break albums of Beethoven
across the back of the john; anyhow, the season
was dragging and the big boys were getting busted,
all the non-pros, the producers, the cameramen,
the pushers of Mary, the fur salesmen, the owners
themselves, and Saint Louie was running this day:
a sidewheeler that broke when he got in close;
he ran with his head down and was mean and ugly
and 35 to 1, and I put a ten down on him.
the driver broke him wide
took him out by the fence where he'd be alone
even if he had to travel four times as far,
and that's the way he went it
all the way by the outer fence
traveling two miles in one
and he won like he was mad as hell
and he wasn't even tired,
and the biggest blonde of all
all ass and breast, hardly anything else
went to the payoff window with me.

that night I couldn't destroy her
although the springs shot sparks
and they pounded on the walls.
later she sat there in her slip
drinking Old Grandad
and she said
what's a guy like you doing
living in a dump like this?

47

and I said
I'm a poet

and she threw back her beautiful head and laughed.

you? you . . . a poet?

I guess you're right, I said, I guess you're right.

but still she looked good to me, she still looked good,
and all thanks to an ugly horse
who wrote this poem.

II

Crucifix
in
a
Deathhand

Poems 1963-1965

the dark is empty;
most of our heroes have been
wrong

view from the screen

I cross the room
to the last wall
the last window
the last pink sun
with its arms around the world
with its arms around me
I hear the death-whisper of the heron
the bone-thoughts of sea-things
that are almost rock;
this screen caved like a soul
and scrawled with flies,
my tensions and damnations
are those of a pig,
pink sun pink sun
I hate your holiness
crawling your gilded cross of life
as my fingers and feet and face
come down to this
sleeping with the whore of your fancy wife
you must some day die for nothing
as I
have lived.

crucifix in a deathhand

yes, they begin out in a willow, I think
the starch mountains begin out in the willow
and keep right on going without regard for
pumas and nectarines
somehow these mountains are like
an old woman with a bad memory and
a shopping basket.
we are in a basin. that is the
idea. down in the sand and the alleys,
this land punched-in, cuffed-out, divided,
held like a crucifix in a deathhand,
this land bought, resold, bought again and
sold again, the wars long over,
the Spaniards all the way back in Spain
down in the thimble again, and now
real estaters, subdividers, landlords, freeway
engineers arguing. this is their land and
I walk on it, live on it a little while
near Hollywood here I see young men in rooms
listening to glazed recordings
and I think too of old men sick of music
sick of everything, and death like suicide
I think is sometimes voluntary, and to get your
hold on the land here it is best to return to the
Grand Central Market, see the old Mexican women,
the poor . . . I am sure you have seen these same women
many years before
arguing
with the same young Japanese clerks
witty, knowledgeable and golden
among their soaring store of oranges, apples
avocados, tomatoes, cucumbers —
and you know how *these* look, they do look good
as if you could eat them all
light a cigar and smoke away the bad world.
then it's best to go back to the bars, the same bars
wooden, stale, merciless, green
with the young policeman walking through
scared and looking for trouble,

and the beer is still bad
it has an edge that already mixes with vomit and
decay, and you've got to be strong in the shadows
to ignore it, to ignore the poor and to ignore yourself
and the shopping bag between your legs
down there feeling good with its avocados and
oranges and fresh fish and wine bottles, who needs
a Fort Lauderdale winter?
25 years ago there used to be a whore there
with a film over one eye, who was too fat
and made little silver bells out of cigarette
tinfoil. the sun seemed warmer then
although this was probably not
true, and you take your shopping bag
outside and walk along the street
and the green beer hangs there
just above your stomach like
a short and shameful shawl, and
you look around and no longer
see any
old men.

grass

at the window
I watch a man with a
power mower
the sounds of his doing race like
flies and bees
on the wallpaper,
it is like a warm fire, and
better than eating steak,
and the grass is green enough
and the sun is sun enough
and what's left of my life
stands there
checking glints of green flying;
it is a giant disrobing of
care, stumbling away from
doing.

suddenly I understand
old men in rockers
bats in Colorado caves
tiny lice crawling into
the eyes of dead birds.

back and forth
he follows his gasoline
sound. it is
interesting enough,
with
the streets
flat on their Spring backs
and smiling.

fuzz

3 small boys run toward me
blowing whistles
and they scream
you're under arrest!
you're drunk!
and they begin
hitting me on the legs with
their toy clubs.
one even has a
badge. another has
handcuffs but my hands are high in the air.

when I go into the liquor store
they whirl around outside
like bees
shut out from their nest.
I buy a fifth of cheap
whiskey
and
3
candy bars.

no lady godiva

she came to my place drunk
riding a deer up on the front porch:
so many women want to save the world
but can't keep their own kitchens straight,
but *me* . . .
we went inside where I lit three red
candles
poured the wine and I took notes on
her:
  latitude behind,
  longitude in
  front. and the
  rest. amaz-
  ing. a woman such as this
  could find
  a zinnia in Hot Springs
  Arkansas.

we ate venison for three weeks.
then she slept with the landlord to help pay
the rent.
then I found her a job as a waitress.
I slept all day and when she came home
I was full of the brilliant conversation that she
so much
adored.

she died quickly one night leaving the world
much the way it had
been.

now I get up early and
go down to the loading docks and wait for
cabbages
oranges
potatoes
to fall from the trucks or to be
thrown away.

by noon I have eaten and am asleep
dreaming of paying the rent
with numbered chunks of plastic
issued by a better
world.

the workers

they laugh continually
even when
a board falls down
and destroys a face
or distorts a
body
they continue to
laugh,
when the color of the eye
becomes a fearful pale
because of the poor
light
they still laugh;
wrinkled and imbecile
at an early age
they joke about it:
a man who looks sixty
will say
I'm 32, and
then they'll laugh
they'll all laugh;
they are sometimes let
outside for a little air
but are chained to return
by chains they would not
break
if they could;
even outside, among
free men
they continue to laugh,
they walk about
with a hobbled and inane
gait
as if they'd lost their
senses; outside
they chew a little bread,
haggle, sleep, count their pennies,
gaze at the clock
and return;

sometimes in the confines
they even grow serious
a moment, they speak of
Outside, of how horrible
it must be
to be
shut *Outside*
forever, never to be let
back in;
it's warm as they work
and they sweat a
bit,
but they work hard and
well, they work so hard
the nerves revolt
and cause trembling,
but often they are
praised by those
who have risen up
out of them
like stars,
and now the stars
watch
watch too
for those few
who might attempt a
slower pace or
show disinterest
or falsify an
illness
in order to gain
rest (rest must be
earned to gain strength
for a more perfect
job).

sometimes one dies
or goes mad
and then from *Outside*
a new one enters

and is given
opportunity.

I have been there
many years;
at first I believed the work
monotonous, even
silly
but now I see
it all has meaning,
and the workers
without faces
I can see are not really
ugly, and that
the heads without eyes —
I know now that those eyes
can see
and are able to
do the work.
the women workers
are often the best,
adapting naturally,
and some of these I
made love to in our
resting hours; at first
they appeared to be
like female apes
but later
with insight
I realized
that they were things
as real and alive as
myself.

the other night
an old worker
grey and blind
no longer useful
was retired

to the *Outside.*

speech! speech!
we demanded.

it was
hell, he said.

we laughed
all 4000 of us:
he had kept his
humor
to the
end.

beans with garlic

this is important enough:
to get your feelings down,
it is better than shaving
or cooking beans with garlic.
it is the little we can do
this small bravery of knowledge
and there is of course
madness and terror too
in knowing
that some part of you
wound up like a clock
can never be wound again
once it stops.
but now
there's a ticking under your shirt
and you whirl the beans with a spoon,
one love dead, one love departed
another love . . .
ah! as many loves as beans
yes, count them now
sad, sad
your feelings boiling over flame,
get this down.

here I am
      in the ground
            my mouth
           open
      and
      I can't even say
         mama,
        and
the dogs run by and stop and piss
on my stone; I get it all
except the sun
and my suit is looking
            bad
and yesterday
        the last of my left
               arm   gone
very little left, all harp-like
without music.

at least a drunk
in bed with a cigarette
might cause 5 fire
          engines and
          33 men.

I can't
    do
      any
        thing.

but p.s. — Hector Richmond in the next
tomb thinks only of Mozart and candy
caterpillars.
    he is
      very bad
        company.

machineguns towers & timeclocks

I feel gypped by dunces
as if reality were the property
of little men
with luck and a headstart,
and I sit in the cold
wondering about purple flowers
along a fence
while the rest of them
stack gold
and Cadillacs and
ladyfriends,
I wonder about palmleaves
and gravestones
and the preciousness of a
cocoon-like sleep;
to be a lizard would be
bad enough
to be scalding in the sun
would be bad enough
but not so bad
as being built up to
Man-size and Man-life
and not wanting the
game, not wanting
machineguns and towers and
timeclocks,
not wanting a carwash
a toothpull
a wristwatch, cufflinks
a pocket radio
tweezers and cotton
a cabinet full of iodine,
not wanting cocktail parties
a front lawn
sing-togethers
new shoes, Christmas presents
life insurance, *Newsweek*
162 baseball games
a vacation in Bermuda.
not wanting not wanting,
and I judge the purple flowers

better off than I
the lizard better off
the dark green hose
the ever grass
the trees the birds,
the cats dreaming in the butter
sun are
better off than
I, getting into this old coat now
feeling for my cigarettes
car keys
a roadmap back,
going out
down the walk
like a man to be executed
walking toward it
surely,
going into it
without guards
driving toward it
racing at it
70 miles per hour,
jockeying
cussing
dropping ashes
deadly ashes of every
deadly thing
burning,
the caterpillar knows less
horror
the armies of ants are
braver
the kiss of a snake
less ravenous,
I only want the sky
to burn me more and more
burn me out
so that the sun begins at
6 in the morning
and goes past midnight
like a drunken door always open,

I drive toward it
not wanting it
getting it getting it
as the cat stretches
yawns
and rolls over into
another dream.

something for the
touts, the nuns, the
grocery clerks
and you . . .

we have everything and we have nothing
and some men do it in churches
and some men do it by tearing butterflies
in half
and some men do it in Palm Springs
laying it into butterblondes
with Cadillac souls
Cadillacs and butterflies
nothing and everything,
the face melting down to the last puff
in a cellar in Corpus Christi.
there's something for the touts, the nuns,
the grocery clerks and you . . .
something at 8 a.m., something in the library
something in the river,
everything and nothing.
in the slaughterhouse it comes running along
the ceiling on a hook, and you swing it —
one
    two
       three
and then you've got it, $200 worth of dead
meat, its bones against your bones
something and nothing.
it's always early enough to die and
it's always too late,
and the drill of blood in the basin white
it tells you nothing at all
and the gravediggers playing poker over
5 a.m. coffee, waiting for the grass
to dismiss the frost . . .
they tell you nothing at all.

we have everything and we have nothing —
days with glass edges and the impossible stink
of river moss — worse than shit;
checkerboard days of moves and countermoves,

fagged interest, with as much sense in defeat as
in victory; slow days like mules
humping it slagged and sullen and sun-glazed
up a road where a madman sits waiting among
bluejays and wrens netted in and sucked a flakey
grey.
good days too of wine and shouting, fights
in alleys, fat legs of women striving around
your bowels buried in moans,
the signs in bullrings like diamonds hollering
Mother Capri, violets coming out of the ground
telling you to forget the dead armies and the loves
that robbed you.
days when children say funny and brilliant things
like savages trying to send you a message through
their bodies while their bodies are still
alive enough to transmit and feel and run up
and down without locks and paychecks and
ideals and possessions and beetle-like
opinions.
days when you can cry all day long in
a green room with the door locked, days
when you can laugh at the breadman
because his legs are too long, days
of looking at hedges . . .

and nothing, and nothing. the days of
the bosses, yellow men
with bad breath and big feet, men
who look like frogs, hyenas, men who walk
as if melody had never been invented, men
who think it is intelligent to hire and fire and
profit, men with expensive wives they possess
like 60 acres of ground to be drilled
or shown-off or to be walled away from
the incompetent, men who'd kill you
because they're crazy and justify it because
it's the law, men who stand in front of
windows 30 feet wide and see nothing,
men with luxury yachts who can sail around

68

the world and yet never get out of their vest
pockets, men like snails, men like eels, men
like slugs, and not as good . . .

and nothing. getting your last paycheck
at a harbor, at a factory, at a hospital, at an
aircraft plant, at a penny arcade, at a
barbershop, at a job you didn't want
anyway.
income tax, sickness, servility, broken
arms, broken heads — all the stuffing
come out like an old pillow.

we have everything and we have nothing.
some do it well enough for a while and
then give way. fame gets them or disgust
or age or lack of proper diet or ink
across the eyes or children in college
or new cars or broken backs while skiing
in Switzerland or new politics or new wives
or just natural change and decay —
the man you knew yesterday hooking
for ten rounds or drinking for three days and
three nights by the Sawtooth mountains now
just something under a sheet or a cross
or a stone or under an easy delusion,
or packing a bible or a golf bag or a
briefcase: how they go, how they go! — all
the ones you thought would never go.

days like this. like your day today.
maybe the rain on the wind6w trying to
get through to you. what do you see today?
what is it? where are you? the best
days are sometimes the first, sometimes
the middle and even sometimes the last.
the vacant lots are not bad, churches in
Europe on postcards are not bad. people in

wax museums frozen into their best sterility
are not bad, horrible but not bad. the
cannon, think of the cannon. and toast for
breakfast the coffee hot enough you
know your tongue is still there. three
geraniums outside a window, trying to be
red and trying to be pink and trying to be
geraniums. no wonder sometimes the women
cry, no wonder the mules don't want
to go up the hill. are you in a hotel room
in Detroit looking for a cigarette? one more
good day. a little bit of it. and as
the nurses come out of the building after
their shift, having had enough, eight nurses
with different names and different places
to go — walking across the lawn, some of them
want cocoa and a paper, some of them want a
hot bath, some of them want a man, some
of them are hardly thinking at all. enough
and not enough. arcs and pilgrims, oranges
gutters, ferns, antibodies, boxes of
tissue paper.

in the most decent sometimes sun
there is the softsmoke feeling from urns
and the canned sound of old battleplanes
and if you go inside and run your finger
along the window ledge you'll find
dirt, maybe even earth.
and if you look out the window
there will be the day, and as you
get older you'll keep looking
keep looking
sucking your tongue in a little
ah ah   no no   maybe

some do it naturally
some obscenely
everywhere.

sway with me

sway with me, everything sad —
madmen in stone houses
without doors,
lepers streaming love and song
frogs trying to figure
the sky;
sway with me, sad things —
fingers split on a forge
old age like breakfast shells
used books, used people
used flowers, used love
I need you
I need you
I need you:
it has run away
like a horse or a dog,
dead or lost
or unforgiving.

lack of almost everything

the essence of the belly
like a white balloon sacked
is disturbing
like the running of feet
on the stairs
when you don't know
who is there.
of course, if you turn on the radio
you might forget
the fat under your shirt
or the rats lined up in order
like old women on Hollywood Blvd
waiting on a comedy
show.
I think of old men
in four dollar rooms
looking for socks in dresser drawers
while standing in brown underwear
all the time the clock ticking on
warm as a
cobra.
ah, there are some decent things, maybe:
the sky, the circus
the legs of ladies getting out of cars,
the peach coming through the door
like a Mozart symphony.
the scale says 198. that's what
I weigh. it is 2:10 a.m.
dedication is for chess players.
the glorious single cause is
waiting on the anvil
while
smoking, pissing, reading Genet
or the funny papers;
but maybe it's early enough yet
to write your aunt in
Palm Springs and tell her
what's wrong.

no. 6

I'll settle for the 6 horse
on a rainy afternoon
a paper cup of coffee
in my hand
a little way to go,
the wind twirling out
small wrens from
the upper grandstand roof,
the jocks coming out
for a middle race
silent
and the easy rain making
everything
at once
almost alike,
the horses at peace with
each other
before the drunken war
and I am under the grandstand
feeling for
cigarettes
settling for coffee,
then the horses walk by
taking their little men
away —
it is funereal and graceful
and glad
like the opening
of flowers.

don't come round but if you do . . .

yeah sure, I'll be in unless I'm out
don't knock if the lights are out
or you hear voices or then
I might be reading Proust
if someone slips Proust under my door
or one of his bones for my stew,
and I can't loan money or
the phone
or what's left of my car
though you can have yesterday's newspaper
an old shirt or a bologna sandwich
or sleep on the couch
if you don't scream at night
and you can talk about yourself
that's only normal;
hard times are upon us all
only I am not trying to raise a family
to send through Harvard
or buy hunting land,
I am not aiming high
I am only trying to keep myself alive
just a little longer,
so if you sometimes knock
and I don't answer
and there isn't a woman in here
maybe I have broken my jaw
and am looking for wire
or I am chasing the butterflies in
my wallpaper,
I mean if I don't answer
I don't answer, and the reason is
that I am not yet ready to kill you
or love you, or even accept you,
it means I don't want to talk
I am busy, I am mad, I am glad
or maybe I'm stringing up a rope;
so even if the lights are on
and you hear sound
like breathing or praying or singing
a radio or the roll of dice
or typing —

go away, it is not the day
the night, the hour;
it is not the ignorance of impoliteness,
I wish to hurt nothing, not even a bug
but sometimes I gather evidence of a kind
that takes some sorting,
and your blue eyes, be they blue
and your hair, if you have some
or your mind — they cannot enter
until the rope is cut or knotted
or until I have shaven into
new mirrors, until the world is
stopped or opened
                    forever.

startled into life like fire

in grievous deity my cat
walks around
he walks around and around
with
electric tail and
push-button
eyes

he is
alive and
plush and
final as a plum tree

neither of us understands
cathedrals or
the man outside
watering his
lawn

if I were all the man
that he is
cat —
if there were men
like this
the world could
begin

he leaps up on the couch
and walks through
porticoes of my
admiration.

stew

stew at noon, my dear; and look:
the ants, the sawdust, the mica
plants, the shadows of banks like
bad jokes;
do you think we'll hear
The Bartered Bride today?
how's your tooth?

I should wash my feet and
clean my nails
not that I'd feel more like Christ
but
less like a leper —
which is important when
poverty is a small game you play
with your time.

let's see: first the mailman
then yesterday's copy of the *Times*.
we might
this way
get blown up a day too
late.

then there's the library or
a walk down the boulevards.

many great men have
walked down the boulevards
but it's terrible to be
a great man

like a monkey carrying a 5 pound
sack of potatoes up a 40 foot hill.

Paris can wait.

more salt?

after we eat
let's sleep, let's sleep.

we can't make any money
awake.

lilies in my brain

the lilies storm my brain
by god by god
like nazi storm troopers!
do you think I'm going
tizzy?

your blue sweater
with tits hanging
loose, and
I think vaguely of Christ
on the cross, I don't know
why, and icecream
cones. this July day
lilies storm my brain,
I'll remember this
but
if only I had a
camera
or a big dog walking beside
me. big dogs make things
concrete
don't they?
a big dog to wrinkle his
snot-nose
like this lake gypped of
clear surface
by a quick and clever
wind.

you're here, yet I'm sad
again. I feel my porkchop ribs
over my lambchop heart *ugh*
gullible hard-working
intestines, dejected penis
chewing-gum bladder
liver turning to fat
like a penny-arcade trout
ashamed buttocks
practical ears

moth-like hands
spearfish nose
rock-slide mouth and
the rest. the rest:
lilies in my brain
hoping good times
thinking old times:
Capone and the diamonds
Charlie Chaplin
Laurel and Hardy
Clara Bow
the rest.

it never happened
but it *seemed* like
there were times when rot
stopped
waited like a streetcar
at a signal.

now I
like a movie punk
(lilies up there)
take your hand
and we walk forward
to rent a boat
to drown in. I breathe the wind, flex my muscles
but only my belly
wiggles.

we get in
the motor churns the
slime.
the city buildings
come down like ostrich
mouths
and hollow out
our brains

yet the sun
comes in
zap! zap! zap!
brilliant germs crawl our
chapped flesh. my
I feel as if I were in
church: everything
stinks. I hold the rubber sides
of everywhere
my balls are snowballs
I see stricken bells of malaria
old men getting into
bed, into model-T Fords
as the fish swim below us
full of dirty words and macaroni
and crossword puzzles
and the death of me, you and
the Katzenjammer
kids.

i am dead but i know
the dead are not like this

the dead can sleep
they don't get up and rage
they don't have a wife.

her white face
like a flower in a closed
window lifts up and
looks at me.

the curtain smokes a cigarette
and a moth dies in a
freeway crash
as I examine the shadows of my
hands.

an owl, the size of a baby clock
rings for me, *come on come on*
it says as Jerusalem is hustled
down crotch-stained halls.

the 5 a.m. grass is nasal now
in hums of battleships and valleys
in the raped light that brings on
the fascist birds.

I put out the lamp and get in bed
beside her, she thinks I'm there
mumbles a rosy gratitude
as I stretch my legs
to coffin length
get in and swim away
from frogs and fortunes.

like a violet in the snow

in the earliest possible day
   in the blue-headed noon
     I will telegraph you
               a
boney hand
         decorated with
sharkskin
      a
       large boy with
yellow teeth and an epileptic
father
     will bring it
           to your
door

    smile
       and
         accept

it is better than
         the
alternative

letter from too far

she wrote me a letter from a small
room near the Seine.
she said she was going to dancing
class. she got up, she said
at 5 o'clock in the morning
and typed at poems
or painted
and when she felt like crying
she had a special bench
by the river.

her book of *Songs*
would be out
in the Fall.

I did not know what to tell her
but
I told her
to get any bad teeth pulled
and be careful of the French
lover.

I put her photo by the radio
near the fan
and it moved
like something
alive.

I sat and watched it
until I had smoked the
5 or 6
cigarettes left.

then I got up
and went to bed.

man in the sun

she reads to me from the *New Yorker*
which I don't buy, don't know
how they get in here, but it's
something about the Mafia
one of the heads of the Mafia
who ate too much and had it too easy
too many fine women patting his
walnuts, and he got fat sucking at good
cigars and young breasts and he
has these heart attacks — and so
one day somebody is driving him
in this big car along the road
and he doesn't feel so good
and he asks the boy to stop and let
him out and the boy lays him out
along the road in the fine sunshine.
I don't know whether it's Crete or
Sicily or Italy proper
but he's lying there in the sunshine
and before he dies he says:
how beautiful life can be, and
then he's gone.

sometimes you've got to kill 4 or 5
thousand men before you somehow
get to believe that the sparrow
is immortal, money is piss and
that you have been wasting
your time.

woman

this head like a saucer
decorated with everything
as lip to lip we hang
in mechanical joy;
my hands blaze with arias
but I think of books
on anatomy,
and I fall from you
as nations burn in anger . . .

to recover from most pitiful error
and rebuild, this is it
loss and mending
until they take us in.

the glory of a Saturday afternoon
like biting into an old peach
and you walk across the room
heavy with everything
except my love.

like all the years wasted

yesterday drunken Alice
gave me
a jar of fig jam
and today she
whistles
for her cat
but
he will not
come —
he is with the horses
at a
tub of beer
or
in room 21
at the Crown Hill
Hotel
or he is at the
Crocker
Citizens National
Bank
or
he arrived in
New York City at
5:30 p.m.
with paper suitcase
and
$7.

next to Alice
in her yard
a paper goose
walks
upside down
on a carton that says:
California
Oranges.

drunken Alice whistles.

no good. no good.
work slowly.
everybody tries hard
but the
gods.

Alice goes in for a
drink, comes
out.
whistles again
all the way to a
park bench in
El Paso —
and her love comes
running out of the
bushes
bright-eyed as a
color film
and not waiting
for
Monday.

we go in
together.

they, all of them, know

ask the sidewalk painters of Paris
ask the sunlight on a sleeping dog
ask the 3 pigs
ask the paperboy
ask the music of Donizetti
ask the barber
ask the murderer
ask the man leaning against a wall
ask the preacher
ask the maker of cabinets
ask the pickpocket or the
       pawnbroker or the glass blower
       or the seller of manure or
       the dentist
ask the revolutionist
ask the man who sticks his head in
       the mouth of a lion
ask the man who will release the next
       atom bomb
ask the man who thinks he's Christ
ask the bluebird who comes home
       at night
ask the peeping Tom
ask the man dying of cancer
ask the man who needs a bath
ask the man with one leg
ask the blind
ask the man with the lisp
ask the opium eater
ask the trembling surgeon
ask the leaves you walk upon
ask a rapist or a
       streetcar conductor or an old man
       pulling weeds in his garden
ask a bloodsucker
ask a trainer of fleas
ask a man who eats fire
ask the most miserable man you can
       find in his most
       miserable moment
ask a teacher of judo

ask a rider of elephants
ask a leper, a lifer, a lunger
ask a professor of history
ask the man who never cleans his
     fingernails
ask a clown or ask the first face you see
     in the light of day
ask your father
ask your son and
     his son to be
ask me
ask a burned-out bulb in a paper sack
ask the tempted, the damned, the foolish
     the wise, the slavering
ask the builders of temples
ask the men who have never worn shoes
ask Jesus
ask the moon
ask the shadows in the closet
ask the moth, the monk, the madman
ask the man who draws cartoons for
     The New Yorker
ask a goldfish
ask a fern shaking to a tapdance
ask the map of India
ask a kind face
ask the man hiding under your bed
ask the man you hate the most in this
     world
ask the man who drank with Dylan Thomas
ask the man who laced Jack Sharkey's gloves
ask the sad-faced man drinking coffee
ask the plumber
ask the man who dreams of ostriches every
     night
ask the ticket-taker at a freak show
ask the counterfeiter
ask the man sleeping in an alley under
     a sheet of paper
ask the conquerors of nations and planets
ask the man who has just cut off his finger

ask a bookmark in the bible
ask the water dripping from a faucet while
    the phone rings
ask perjury
ask the deep blue paint
ask the parachute jumper
ask the man with the bellyache
ask the divine eye so sleek and swimming
ask the boy wearing tight pants in
    the expensive academy
ask the man who slipped in the bathtub
ask the man chewed by the shark
ask the one who sold me the unmatched
    gloves
ask these and all those I have left out
ask the fire the fire the fire —
ask even the liars
ask anybody you please at anytime
    you please on any day you please
    whether it's raining or whether
    the snow is there or whether
    you are stepping out onto a porch
    yellow with warm heat
ask this ask that
ask the man with birdshit in his hair
ask the torturer of animals
ask the man who has seen many bullfights
    in Spain
ask the owners of new Cadillacs
ask the famous
ask the timid
ask the albino
    and the statesman
ask the landlords and the poolplayers
ask the phonies
ask the hired killers
ask the bald men and the fat men
    and the tall men and the
    short men
ask the one-eyed men, the
    oversexed and undersexed men

ask the men who read all the newspaper
    editorials
ask the men who breed roses
ask the men who feel almost no pain
ask the dying
ask the mowers of lawns and the attenders
    of football games
ask any of these or all of these
ask ask ask and
    they'll all tell you:

a snarling wife on the balustrade is more
than a man can bear.

a nice day

the virus holds
the concepts give way like rotten
shoelaces
toothache and bacon dance on the
lawn
I open a drawer to dirty
stockings
a stockbroker's universe
steel balls flutter like
butterflies
I can feel doom like
something under the sheets with bristles
that stinks and moves
toward me
the mailman is insane and
hands me a bagful of snails
eaten inside
out
by some rat of decay
in the madhouse a man kisses the walls
and dreams of sailboating down some
cool Nile
I read about the bullfights the ballgames
the boxing matches
things continue to fight
and in the churches they play at parlor
games and peek at legs
I go outside to absolutely
nothing
a square round of orange zero
headpieces over obscene mouths that form
at me like suckerfish
        good morning, nice day isn't it?
        a fat woman says
I am unable to answer
and down the sidewalk I go
shamed
unable to tell her
of the knife inside me
I do notice though the sun is shining
that the flowers are pulled up on

their strings
and I on mine:
belly, bellybutton, buttocks, bukowski
waving walking
teeth of ice with the taste of tar
tear ducts propagandized
shoes acting like shoes
I arrive on time
in the blazing midday of
mourning.

III

At Terror Street
and Agony Way

Poems 1965-1968

*it was a splendid day in Spring
and outside we could hear the birds
that hadn't been killed
by the smog*

beerbottle

a very miraculous thing just happened:
my beerbottle flipped over backwards
and landed on its bottom on the floor,
and I have set it upon the table to foam down,
but the photos were not so lucky today
and there is a small slit along the leather
of my left shoe, but it's all very simple:
we cannot acquire too much: there are laws
we know nothing of, all manner of nudges
set us to burning or freezing; what sets
the blackbird in the cat's mouth
is not for us to say, or why some men
are jailed like pet squirrels
while others nuzzle in enormous breasts
through endless nights — this is the
task and the terror, and we are not
taught why. still, it's lucky the bottle
landed straightside up, and although
I have one of wine and one of whiskey,
this foretells, somehow, a good night,
and perhaps tomorrow my nose will be longer:
new shoes, less rain, more poems.

the body

I have been
hanging here
headless
for so long
that the body has forgotten
why
or where or when it
happened

and the toes
walk along in shoes
that do not
care

and although
the fingers
slice things and
hold things and
move things and
touch
things
such as
oranges
apples
onions
books
bodies
I am no longer
reasonably sure
what these things
are

they are mostly
like
lamplight and
fog

then often the hands will
go to the
lost head
and hold the head
like the hands of a
child
around a ball
a block
air and wood —
no teeth
no thinking part

and when a window
blows open
to a
church
hill
woman
dog
or something singing

the fingers of the hand
are senseless to vibration
because they have no
ears
senseless to color because
they have no
eyes
senseless to smell
without a nose

the country goes by as
nonsense
the continents

the daylights and evenings
shine

on my dirty
fingernails

and in some mirror
my face
a block to vanish
scuffed part of a child's
ball

while everywhere
moves
worms and aircraft
fires on the land
tall violets in sanctity
my hands let go let go
let go

k.o.

he was easy, fat as a hummingbird
and I had him blowing,
I jabbed and crossed and took my time:
everybody was waiting for the main event,
drinking beer, and I was thinking
how we were going to furnish the house,
I needed a workbench and some tools,
and then he came over with the right —
I had been looking at the lights
and the next thing I knew everybody was
howling, and I was down on my knees like
praying, and when I got up
he was strong and I was weak;
well, I thought, I'll go back to the farm,
I always was a poor winner.

sunday before noon

spinach, Gabriel,
all fall down,
all fall down and blow,
barbados, barbados,
where are yr toes?

the branches break, the birds fall, the buildings burn,
the whores stand straight,
the bombs stack,
evening, morning, night,
peanutbutter,
peanutbutter falcons,
rain breathing like lilies from the top of my head,
pincers pincers
kisses like steel clamps
mouths full of moths,
hydra-headed cocksuckers,
Florida in full moon,
shark with mouthful of man
man with mouthful of peanutbutter, rain
rain peeking into the guts of grey hours,
horses dreaming of horses,
flowers dreaming of flowers,
horses running with greyhour pieces of my lovely flesh,
bread burning, all Spain on fire and
cities dreaming of craters,
bombs bigger than the brains of anything,
going down
are the clocks cocks roosters?
the roosters stand on the fence
the roosters are peanutbutter crowing,
the FLAME will be high, the flame will be big,
kiss kiss kiss
everything away,
I hope it rains today, I hope
the jets die, I hope
the kitten finds a mouse, I hope
I don't see it, I hope
it rains, I hope

anything away from here,
I hope a bridge, a fish, a cactus somewhere
strutting whiskers to the noon,
I dream flowers and horses
the branches break the birds fall the buildings
burn, my whore walks across the room and
smiles at me.

7th race when the
angels swung low and burned

I watched the board and the 6 dropped to 9
after a first flash of 18 from a morning line
of 12 . . . two minutes to post and a fat man
kept jamming against my back, but I made it,
I bet 20 to win and walked out to the deck
looking down at my program:
purple and cerise quarters, cerise sleeves
and cap; b.f.3., Indian Red — Impetuous, by Top Row,
and people kept walking into me
although there was no place to go,
they were putting them in the gate
and the people were walking like ants over spilled
sugar,
the machine had cranked them up to die
and they were blind with it,
and now by the 7th race
stinking sweating broke ugly
reamed
there was no way back to the dream,
and the horses came out of the gate
and I looked for my colors —
I saw them, and the boy seemed to be riding sideways
he had the horse running in and was pulling his head back
toward the outer rail,
and I could tell by the way the horse was striding
that he was out of it;
the action had been all wrong
and I walked to the bar
while the winners turned into the stretch,
and they were making the final calls as I ordered my drink,
and I leaned there thinking
I once knew places that sweetly cried
their walls' voices
where mirrors showed me chance,
I was once saddened when an evening became
finally a night to sleep away.

— the bartender said, I hear they are going to send in
the 7 horse in the next one.

I once sang operas and burned candles
in a place made holy by nothing but myself
and whatever there was.

— I never bet mares in the summer,
I told him.

then the crowd came on in
complaining
explaining
bragging
thinking of suicide or drunkenness or sex,
and I looked around
like a man waking up in jail
and whatever there was
became that,
and I finished my drink
and walked away.

on going out to get the mail

the droll noon
where squadrons of worms creep up like
stripteasers
to be raped by blackbirds.

I go outside
and all up and down the street
the green armies shoot color
like an everlasting 4th of July,
and I too seem to swell inside,
a kind of unknown bursting, a
feeling, perhaps, that there isn't any
enemy
anywhere.

and I reach down into the box
and there is
nothing — not even a
letter from the gas co. saying they will
shut it off
again.

not even a short note from my x-wife
bragging about her present
happiness.

my hand searches the mailbox in a kind of
disbelief long after the mind has
given up.

there's not even a dead fly
down in there.

I am a fool, I think, I should have known it
works like this.

I go inside as all the flowers leap to
please me.

anything? the woman
asks.

nothing, I answer, what's for
breakfast?

i wanted to overthrow the
government
but all i brought down was somebody's wife

30 dogs, 20 men on 20 horses and one fox
and look here, they write,
you are a dupe for the state, the church,
you are in the ego-dream,
read your history, study the monetary system,
note that the racial war is 23,000 years old.

well, I remember 20 years ago, sitting with an old Jewish tailor,
his nose in the lamplight like a cannon sighted on the enemy; and
there was an Italian pharmacist who lived in an expensive apartment
in the best part of town; we plotted to overthrow
a tottering dynasty, the tailor sewing buttons on a vest,
the Italian poking his cigar in my eye, lighting me up,
a tottering dynasty myself, always drunk as possible,
well-read, starving, depressed, but actually
a good young piece of ass would have solved all my rancor,
but I didn't know this; I listened to my Italian and my Jew
and I went out down dark alleys smoking borrowed cigarettes
and watching the backs of houses come down in flames,
but somewhere we missed: we were not men enough,
     large or small enough,
or we only wanted to talk or we were bored, so the anarchy
     fell through,
and the Jew died and the Italian grew angry because I stayed
     with his
wife when he went down to the pharmacy; he did not care to have
his *personal* government overthrown, and she overthrew easy, and
I had some guilt: the children were asleep in the other bedroom;
but later I won $200 in a crap game and took a bus to New Orleans,
and I stood on the corner listening to the music coming from bars
and then I went inside to the bars,
and I sat there thinking about the dead Jew,
how all he did was sew on buttons and talk,
and how he gave way although he was stronger than any of us —
he gave way because his bladder would not go on,
and maybe that saved Wall Street and Manhattan
and the Church and Central Park West and Rome and the
Left Bank, but the pharmacist's wife, she was nice,

she was tired of bombs under the pillow and hissing the Pope,
and she had a very nice figure, very good legs,
but I guess she felt as I: that the weakness was not Government
but Man, one at a time, that men were never as strong as
    their ideas
and that ideas were governments turned into men;
and so it began on a couch with a spilled martini
and it ended in the bedroom: desire, revolution,
nonsense ended, and the shades rattled in the wind,
rattled like sabres, cracked like cannon,
and 30 dogs, 20 men on 20 horses chased one fox
across the fields under the sun,
and I got out of bed and yawned and scratched my belly
and knew that soon   very soon   I would have to get
very drunk   again.

the girls

I have been looking at
the same
lampshade
for
    5 years
and it has gathered
a bachelor's dust
and
the girls who enter here
are too
busy
to clean it

but I don't mind
I have been too
busy
to notice
until now

that the light
shines
badly
        through
     5 years'
worth.

a note on rejection slips

it is not very good
to not get through
whether it's the
wall
the human mind
sleep
wakefulness
sex
excretion
or most anything
you can name
or
can't name.

when a chicken
catches its worm
the chicken gets through
and when the worm
catches you
(dead or alive)
I'd have to say,
even through its lack
of sensibility,
that it enjoys
it.

it's like when you
send this poem
back
I'll figure
it just didn't get
through.

either there were
fatter worms
or the chicken
couldn't
see.

the next time
I break an egg
I'll think of
you.

scramble with
fork

and then turn up
the flame

if I
have
one.

true story

they found him walking along the freeway
all red in
front
he had taken a rusty tin can
and cut off his sexual
machinery
as if to say —
see what you've done to
me? you might as well have the
rest.

and he put part of him
in one pocket and
part of him in
another
and that's how they found him,
walking
along.

they gave him over to the
doctors
who tried to sew the parts
back
on
but the parts were
quite contented
they way they
were.

I think sometimes of all the good
ass
turned over to the
monsters of the
world.

maybe it was his protest against
this or

his protest
against
everything.

a one man
Freedom March
that never squeezed in
between
the concert reviews and the
baseball
scores.

God, or somebody,
bless
him.

x-pug

he hooked to the body hard
took it well
and loved to fight
had seven in a row and a small fleck
over one eye,
and then he met a kid from Camden
with arms thin as wires —
it was a good one,
the safe lions roared and threw money;
they were both up and down many times,
but he lost that one
and he lost the rematch
in which neither of them fought at all,
hanging on to each other like lovers through the boos,
and now he's over at Mike's
changing tires and oil and batteries,
the fleck over the eye
still young,
but you don't ask him,
you don't ask him anything
except maybe
you think it's going to rain?
or
you think the sun's gonna come out?
to which he'll usually answer
hell no,
but you'll have your important tank of gas
and drive off.

class

these boys have got class
they ought to make kings
out of old men
rolling cigarettes
in rooms small enough
to recognize
a single shadow;
for them
all has gone away
like a light under the
door
yet
they recognize and
bear the absence;
tricked and slugged to
zero
they wait on death
with the temperate patience of
a mother teaching her child
to eat;
for them, everything has
run away
like a rose in the mouth
of a hog;
the burning of cities
must have been
like this.
but like trucks of garbage
shaking with love
these boys
might
rise like Lorca
out of the road
with one more poem,
rise like
Lazarus to
gaze upon the
still living female,
and then
get drunk
drunk

until it all
falls apart
so sad
again.

living

I mean, I just slept
I awoke with a fly on my elbow and
I named the fly Benny
then I killed him
and then I got up and looked in the
mailbox
and there was some kind of warning from the
government
but since there wasn't anybody standing in the bushes with
a bayonet
I tore it up
and went back to bed and looked up at the ceiling
and I thought, I really like this,
I'm just going to lie here for another ten
minutes
and I lay there for another ten minutes
and I thought,
it doesn't make sense, I've got so many things to
do but I'm going to lie here another
half hour,
and I stretched
          stretched
and I watched the sun through the small leaves of a tree
outside, and I didn't have any wonderful thoughts,
I didn't have any immortal thoughts,
and that was the best part
and it got a little hot
and I threw the blankets off and slept —
but a damned dream:
I was on the train again
on that same 5 hour round-trip to the track,
sitting by the window,
past the same sad ocean, China out there mouthing
peculiarities in the back of my
brain, and then somebody sat next to me
and talked about *horses*
mothballs of talk that ripped me apart like
death, and then I was there
again: the horses running like something shown on a
screen and the jockeys very white in the face
and it didn't matter who finally

118

won and everybody knew
it, the ride back in the dream was the same as the ride
back in reality:
black tons of night around
the same mountains ashamed of being
there, the sea again, again,
the train heading like a cock through a needle's
eye
and I had to get up and go to the urinal
and I hated to get up and go to the urinal
because somebody had thrown paper, some loser had thrown paper
into the toilet again and it wouldn't
flush, and when I came back out
everybody had nothing to do but look at my
face
and I am so tired
that they know when they see my face
that I hate
them
and then they hate me
and want to
kill me
but don't.
            I woke up but since there wasn't anybody
            over my bed
            to tell me I was doing
            wrong
            I slept some
            more.
when I woke up this time
it was almost
evening. people were coming in from work.
I got up and sat in a chair and watched them
coming in. they didn't look so good.
even the young girls didn't look so good as when they
left.
and the men came in: hatchet men, killers, thieves, con-men,
the whole bunch, and their faces were more horrible than any
halloween masks ever devised.

I found a blue spider in the corner and killed him with a
broom.

I looked at the people a while more and then I got tired and
stopped looking and fried myself a couple of eggs and sat down
and had some tea and bread with it.

I felt fine.

then I took a bath and went back to
bed.

the intellectual

she writes
continually
like a long nozzle
spraying
the air,
and she argues
continually;
there is nothing
I can say
that is really not'
something else,
so,
I stop saying;
and finally
she argues herself
out the door
saying
something like —
I'm not *trying* to
impress myself
upon you.

but I know
she will be
back, they always
come back.

and
at 5 p.m.
she was knocking at the door.

I let her in.

I won't stay long, she said,
if you don't want me.

it's all right, I said,
I've got to take a
bath.

she walked into the kitchen and
began on the
dishes.

it's like being married:
you accept
everything
as if
it hadn't happened.

shot of red-eye

I used to hold my social security card
up in the air,
he told me,
but I was so small
they couldn't see it,
all those big
guys around.

you mean the place with the
big green screen?
I asked.

yeah. well, anyhow, I finally got on
the other day
picking tomatoes, and Jesus Christ,
I couldn't get anywhere
it was too hot, too hot
and I couldn't get anything in my sack
so I lay under the truck
in the shade and drank
wine. I didn't make a
dime.

have a drink, I said.

sure, he said.

two big women came in and
I mean BIG
and they sat next to
us.

shot of red-eye, one of them
said to the bartender.

likewise, said the other.

they pulled their dresses up
around their hips and
swung their legs.

um, umm. I think I'm going mad, I told
my friend from the tomato fields.

Jesus, he said, Jesus and Mary, I can't
believe what I see.

it's all
there, I said.

you a fighter? the one next to me
asked.

no, I said.

what happened to your
face?

automobile accident on the San Berdoo
freeway. some drunk jumped the divider. I was
the drunk.

how old *are* you, daddy?

old enough to slice the melon, I said,
tapping my cigar ashes into my beer to give me
strength.

can you buy a melon? she asked.

have you ever been chased across the Mojave and
raped?

no, she said.

I pulled out my last 20 and with an old man's
virile abandon ordered
four drinks.

both girls smiled and pulled their dresses
higher, if that was possible.

who's your friend? they asked.

this is Lord Chesterfield, I told them.

pleased ta meetcha, they
said.

hello, bitches, he answered.

we walked through the 3rd street tunnel
to a green hotel. the girls had a
key.

there was one bed and we all got
in. I don't know who got
who.

125

the next morning my friend and I
were down at the Farm Labor Market
on San Pedro Street
holding up and waving our social
security cards.

they couldn't see
his.

I was the last one on the truck out. a big woman stood
up against me. she smelled like
port wine.

honey, she asked, whatever happened to your
face?

fair grounds, a dancing bear who
didn't.

bullshit, she said.

maybe so, I said, but get your hand out
from around my
balls. everybody's looking.

when we got to the
fields the sun was
really up
and the world
looked
terrible.

i met a genius

I met a genius on the train
today
about 6 years old,
he sat beside me
and as the train
ran down along the coast
we came to the ocean
and then he looked at me
and said,
it's not pretty.

it was the first time I'd
realized
that.

poverty

it is the man you've never seen who
keeps you going,
the one who might arrive
someday.

he isn't out on the streets or
in the buildings or in the
stadiums,
or if he's there
I've missed him somehow.

he isn't one of our presidents
or statesmen or actors.

I wonder if he's there.

I walk down the streets
past drugstores and hospitals and
theatres and cafes
and I wonder if he is there.

I have looked almost half a century
and he has not been seen.

a living man, truly alive,
say when he brings his hands down
from lighting a cigarette
you see his eyes
like the eyes of a tiger staring past
into the wind.

but when the hands come down
it is always the
other eyes

that are there
always always.

and soon it will be too late for me
and I will have lived a life
with drugstores, cats, sheets, saliva,
newspapers, women, doors and other assortments,
but nowhere
a living man.

to kiss the worms goodnight

kool enough to die but not
kill I take my doctor's green
pill
drink tea
as the sharks swim through vases of
flowers
ten times around they go
twenty
searching for my sissy
heart
in a freak May night in
Los Angeles
Sunday
somebody playing
Beethoven

I sit behind pulled shades
in ambush
as ambitious men with new automobiles and
new blondes
command the streets
I sit in a rented room
carving a wooden rifle
drawing pictures of naked ladies
bulls
love affairs
old men
on the walls with children's
crayons
it is up to each of us to live in
whatever way we can
as the generals, doctors, policemen
warn and torture
us

I bathe once a day
am frightened by cats and
shadows
sleep hardly at all

when my heart stops
the whole world will get quicker
better
warmer
summer will follow summer
the air will be lake clear
and the meaning
too

but meanwhile
the green pill
these greasy floors off the
avenue and
down there a plot of worms of worms of
worms
and up here
no nymph blonde
to love me to sleep while I am
waiting.

john dillinger and *le chasseur maudit*

it's unfortunate, and simply not the style, but I don't care:
girls remind me of hair in the sink, girls remind me of intestines
and bladders and excretory movements; it's unfortunate also that
ice-cream bells, babies, engine-valves, plagiostomes, palm trees,
footsteps in the hall . . . all excite me with the cold calmness
of the gravestone; nowhere, perhaps, is there sanctuary except
in hearing that there were other desperate men:
Dillinger, Rimbaud, Villon, Babyface Nelson, Seneca, Van Gogh,
or desperate women: lady wrestlers, nurses, waitresses, whores
poetesses . . . although,
I do suppose the breaking out of ice-cubes is important
or a mouse nosing an empty beercan —
two hollow emptinesses looking into each other,
or the nightsea stuck with soiled ships
that enter the chary web of your brain with their lights,
with their salty lights
that touch you and leave you
for the more solid love of some India;
or driving great distances without reason
sleep-drugged through open windows that
tear and flap your shirt like a frightened bird,
and always the stoplights, always red,
nightfire and defeat, defeat . . .
scorpions, scraps, fardels:
x-jobs, x-wives, x-faces, x-lives,
Beethoven in his grave as dead as a beet;
red wheel-barrows, yes, perhaps,
or a letter from Hell signed by the devil
or two good boys beating the guts out of each other
in some cheap stadium full of screaming smoke,
but mostly, I don't care, sitting here
with a mouthful of rotten teeth,
sitting here reading Herrick and Spenser and
Marvell and Hopkins and Bronte (Emily, today);
and listening to the Dvorak *Midday Witch*
or Franck's *Le Chasseur Maudit*,
actually I don't care, and it's unfortunate:
I have been getting letters from a young poet
(very young, it seems) telling me that some day
I will most surely be recognized as
one of the world's great poets. *Poet!*

a malversation: today I walked in the sun and streets
of this city: seeing nothing, learning nothing, being
nothing, and coming back to my room
I passed an old woman who smiled a horrible smile;
she was already dead, and everywhere I remembered wires:
telephone wires, electric wires, wires for electric faces
trapped like goldfish in the glass and smiling,
and the birds were gone, none of the birds wanted wire
or the smiling of wire
and I closed my door (at last)
but through the windows it was the same:
a horn honked, somebody laughed, a toilet flushed,
and oddly then
I thought of all the horses with numbers
that have gone by in the screaming,
gone by like Socrates, gone by like Lorca,
like Chatterton . . .
I'd rather imagine our death will not matter too much
except as a matter of disposal, a problem,
like dumping the garbage,
and although I have saved the young poet's letters,
I do not believe them
but like at the
diseased palm trees
and the end of the sun,
I sometimes look.

the flower lover

in the Valkerie Mountains
among the strutting peacocks
I found a flower
as large as my
head
and when I reached in to smell
it

I lost an ear lobe
part of my nose
one eye
and half a pack of
cigarettes.

I came back
the next day
to hack the damned thing
down
but found it so
beautiful I
killed a
peacock
instead.

traffic ticket

I walked off the job again
and the police stopped me
for running a red light at Serrano Ave.
my mind was rather gone
and I stood in a patch of leaves
ankle-deep
and kept my head turned
so they couldn't smell the liquor
too much
and I took the ticket and went to my room
and got a good symphony on the radio,
one of the Russians or Germans,
one of the dark tough boys
but still I felt lonely and cold
and kept lighting cigarettes
and I turned on the heater
and then down on the floor
I saw a magazine with my photo
on the cover
and I walked over and picked it up
but it wasn't me
because yesterday is gone
and today is only catsup
and racing hounds
and sickness
and women some women
momentarily as beautiful
as any of the cathedrals,
and now they play Bartok
who knew what he was doing
which meant he didn't know what he was doing,
and tomorrow I suppose I will go back
to the fucking job
like a man to a wife with four kids
if they'll have me
but today I know that I have gotten out of
some kind of net,
30 seconds more and I would have been dead,
and it is important to recognize
one should recognize
that type of moment

if he wants to continue
to avail the gut and the sacked skull of a
flower   a mountain   a ship   a woman
the code of the frost and the stone
everything lapsing into a sense of moment
that cleans like the best damn soap on the market
and brings Paris, Spain, the groans of Hemingway,
the blue madonna, the new-born bull,
a night in a closet with red paint
right down in on you,
and I hope to pay the ticket
even though I did not (I think) run the red light
but
they said I did.

a little sleep and peace of stillness

if you're a man, Los Angeles is where you hang it up and
battle; or if you're a woman, and you've got enough leg and
the rest, you sail it against a mountain backdrop so
when you grow grey you can hide in Beverly Hills
in a mansion so nobody can see how you've decayed.
so we moved here — and what do we come up against
except a religious maniac in the next shack who
drinks cheap wine and has visions and plays his radio
as loudly as possible, my god!
I know all the spirituals now!
I know how very much I have sinned and I realize I must die
and I've got to get ready . . .
but I could use a little sleep first
just a little sleep and peace of silence.

I open the window and there he is
out on the lawn
dancing to a hymn
a spiritual
a whatever.
he has on a pair of red bathing trunks
he's well-tanned and drunk on wine
but his movements are hard and awkward —
he's too fat
a walnut-like man, distorted and shapeless at
55.
and he waves his arms in the sun and the birds fly up
frightened
and then he whirls back into his doorway.

but the view from the street here is good —
there are Japanese and old women and young girls and
beggars.
we have large palms
plenty of birds
and the parking's not bad . . .
but our religious maniac does not work
he's too clever to work
and so we both lie around

listen to his radio
drink
and I wonder which of us will get to hell first —
him with his bible or me with my Racing Form
but if I've got to hear him down there I know I'm going to have to
have some help, and the next dance will be mine.

right now I wish I had something to sell so I could hide in a
      place
with walls twelve feet high
with moats
and high-yellow mamas.
but it looks like some long days and nights ahead,
as always.
at the least I can only hope for the weakening of a
radio tube,
and at the most for his death,
which we are both praying and
ready for.

he even looked like a nice guy

he packaged it up neatly in different sections
sending the legs to an aunt in St. Louis
the head to a scoutmaster in Brooklyn
the belly to a cross-eyed butcher in Des Moines,
the female organs were sent to a young priest in Los Angeles;
the arms he threw to his dog
and he kept the hands to use as nut-crackers, and all the
leftover and assorted parts
like breasts and buttocks he boiled into a soup
which strangely
tasted better than she ever had.

he spent the money in her purse
he bought good French wine, frijoles, a pound of grass
and two parakeets; he bought the collected works of
Keats, a 5 foot square red bandana, a scissors with
ivory handles, and a box of candy for his
landlady.

then he drank and ate and slept for three days and nights
and when the police came
he seemed very friendly and calm
and all the way to the station house
he talked of the weather, the color of the mountains,
various things like that, he didn't seem like that kind of killer
at all.

it was very strange.

the boys come up
the boys climb up the
brown pole
as the waterheater gurgles
in Spanish
the boys climb the
brown pole —

Charlemagne fought for this
Il Duce was tilted from his car
skinned like a bear
and hung
upsidedown
for this —

the boys climb up
the brown pole
3 or 4 of
them;
we have just moved in
this building,
the paintings still
unpacked, the letters from
England and Chicago and
Cheyenne and
New Orleans,
but the beer's on
and there are 5 oranges
and 4 pears on the table
so life's not
bad
except somebody wanted
$15 to
turn on the gas;
the boys climb the phonepole
to leap onto the
bluegreen
garage roofs
and I stand naked
behind a curtain,
smoking a cigar,

and impressed
impressed as I can be
as if
the Virgin Mary
was dancing
outside;
and through the window
to the North
I can see 2 men
feeding
45 pigeons
and the pigeons
walk in separate circles
of 8 or 10
as if tied together
by a revolving string,
and it is 3 o'clock
in the afternoon and
a good cigar.

Cicero fought for this,
Jake LaMotta and
Waslaw Nijinsky,
but somebody stole
our guitar
and I haven't taken my
vitamins
for weeks.

the boys run on the
greenblue roofs
as to the North the
pigeons rise;
it is desperately
holy
and I blow out
grey and quiet
smoke.

then a woman in a red coat,
evidently an official,
some matron of
learning
decides that
the sky needs
cleaning:

    Hey ! ! !   you boys get
        DOWN
from there!

it is beautiful as
deer
running from the
hunter.

Agrippina fought for this,
even Mithridates,
even William Hazlitt.

there is nothing to do
now
but unpack.

the weather is hot on the back of my watch

the weather is hot on the back of my watch
which is down at Finkelstein's
who is gifted with 3 balls
but no heart, but you've got to understand
when the bull goes down
or the whore, the heart is laid aside for something else,
and let's not over-rate obvious decency
for in a crap game you may be cutting down
some wobbly king of 6 kids
and a hemorrhoid butt on his last unemployment check,
and who is to say the rose is greater than the thorn?
not I, Henry,
and when your love gets flabby knees and prefers flat shoes,
maybe you should have stuck it into something else
like an oil well
or a herd of cows.
I'm too old to argue,
I've gone with the poem
and been k.o.'d with the old sucker-punch
round after round,
but sometimes I like to think of the Kaiser
or any other fool full of medals and nothing else,
or the first time we read Dos
or Eliot with his trousers rolled;
the weather is hot on the back of my watch
which is down at Finkelstein's,
but you know what they say: things are tough all over,
and I remember once on the bum in Texas
I watched a crow-blast, one hundred farmers with one hundred
    shotguns
jerking off the sky with a giant penis of hate
and the crows came down half-dead, half-living,
and they clubbed them to death to save their shells
but they ran out of shells before they ran out of crows
and the crows came back and walked around the pellets and
stuck out their tongues
and mourned their dead and elected new leaders
and then all at once flew home to fuck to fill the gap.

you can only kill what shouldn't be there,

143

and Finkelstein should be there and my watch
and maybe myself, and I realize that if the poems are bad
they are supposed to be bad and if they are good
they are likewise supposed to be — although there is a minor
fight to be fought,
but still I am sad
because I was in this small town somewhere in the badlands,
way off course, not even wanting to be there,
two dollars in my wallet, and a farmer turned to me
and asked me what time it was
and I wouldn't tell him,
and later they gathered them up for burning
as if they were no better than dung with feathers,
feathers and a little gasoline,
and from the bottom of one pile
a not-quite-dead crow smiled at me.

it was 4:35 p.m.

note to a lady who expected rupert brooke

wha', what *did* you expect? a schoolboy lisping Donne? or
some more practical lover filling you with the stench of Life?
I'm a fool and no gentleman: I walked the Brooklyn Bridge
with Crane in pajamas, but suicide fails as you get older:
there's less and less to kill.

so among the skin and lambchops, the sick neckties of
other closets, I scheme schemes round as oranges
filled with the music of my crafty mumbling.

Brooke? no. I am a monkey with an olive lost in the
circus sand of your laughter, circus apes, circus tigers,
circus madmen of finance screwing their secretaries before
the 5:15 . . . and what did *you* expect?

a pink-cheek dribbling Picasso colors on your dry brain?

so, the room was blue with the smoke of my boiling, hell,
a senseless sea
and I fell fingers sotted to the last pinch of your juice,
fell through the thorned vines cursing your name,
no gentleman
no gentleman,
kissed-off love like snake-bite,
the veranda buzzed with flies, buzzed with flies
and lies, and your red mouth screamed,
            your lamps screamed
breaking like overdue bills:

        DRUNK! DRUNK AGAIN!
        O, YOU IDIOT!

so, Yeats, Keats, teats . . . nothing but an apricot!

145

wha', what happened to Spain? my boy Lorca?
the revolution? must join the brigade!
lemme outa here!

the difference between a
bad poet and a good one is luck

I suppose so.
I was living in an attic in Philadelphia
it became very hot in the summer and so I stayed in the
bars. I didn't have any money and so with what was almost left
I put a small ad in the paper and said I was a writer
looking for work . . .
which was a god damned lie; I was a writer
looking for a little time and a little food and some
attic rent.
a couple of days later when I finally came home
from somewhere
the landlady said, there was somebody looking for
you. and I said,
there must be some mistake. she said,
no, it was a writer and he said he wanted you to help him write
a history book:
oh, fine, I said, and I knew with that I had another week's
rent — I mean, on the cuff —
so I sat around drinking wine on credit and watching the
    hot pigeons
suffer and fuck on my hot roof.
I turned the radio on real loud
drank the wine and wondered how I could make a history book
interesting but true.
but the bastard never came back,
and I had to finally sign on with a railroad track gang
going West
and they gave us cans of food but no
openers
and we broke the cans against the seats and sides of
railroad cars a hundred years old with dust
the food wasn't cooked and the water tasted like
candlewick
and I leaped off into a clump of brush somewhere in
Texas
all green with nice-looking houses in the
distance
I found a park
slept all night
and then they found me and put me in a cell

147

and they asked me about murders and
robberies.
they wanted to get a lot of stuff off the books
to prove their efficiency
but I wasn't *that* tired
and they drove me to the next big town
fifty-seven miles away
the big one kicked me in the ass
and they drove off.
but I lucked it:
two weeks later I was sitting in the office of the city hall
half-asleep in the sun like the big fly on my elbow
and now and then she took me down to a meeting of the council
and I listened very gravely as if I knew what was happening
as if I knew how the funds of a halfass town were being
dismantled.
later I went to bed and woke up with teethmarks all over
me, and I said, Christ, watch it, baby! you might give me
cancer! and I'm rewriting the history of the Crimean War!
and they all came to her house —
all the cowboys, all the cowboys:
fat, dull and covered with dust.
and we all shook hands.
I had on a pair of old bluejeans, and they said
oh, you're a writer, eh?
and I said: well, some think so.
and some still think so . . .
others, of course, haven't quite wised up yet.
two weeks later they
ran me out
of town.

the curtains are waving and people walk through the afternoon
here and in Berlin and in New York City and in Mexico

I wait on life like a pregnancy, put the stethoscope to
the gut
but all I hear now is
the piano slamming its teeth through areas of my
brain
      (somebody in this neighborhood likes
      Gershwin which is too bad
      for
         me)
and the woman sits behind me
sits there sits there
and keeps lighting cigarettes
and now the nurses leave the hospital near here
and they wear dresses that are naked in the sun
to cheer the dead and the dying and the doctors
but it does not help
me
   if I could rip them with moans of delight it
   would neither add or take away
   anything

      now now

          a horn blows a tired
summer like a gladiola given up and leaning against a
house and
the bottles we have emptied would strangle the
sensibilities . . . of God

now I look up and see my face in the mirror:
if I could only kill the man who killed the
man

more than coffeepots and cheroots have done me
in   more than myself has done me

in

madness comes like a mouse out of the cupboard and
they hand me a photograph of the
moon

the woman behind me has a daughter who falls in love
with men in beards and sandals and berets
who smoke pipes and carefully comb their hair and
play chess and talk continually of the
soul and of Art

this is good enough: you've got to love
something

now the landlord waters outside dripping the
plants with false rain
Gershwin is finished now it sounds like
Greig

o, it's all so common and hard! impossible!
I do wish somebody would go blackberry
wild

but no
I suppose it will be the
same: a beer and then another
        beer and then another
        beer
maybe then a halfpint of
scotch
three cigars — smoke smoke yes smoke
under the electric sun of night
hidden here in these walls with this woman and her
life while

the police are taking the drunks off the
streets

I do not know how much longer I can
last
but I keep thinking
      ow!   my god!
                    the
gladiola will straighten hard and
full of
color like an
arrow pointing at the
sun
Christ will shudder like
marmalade
my cat will look like Gandhi once
looked
      everything everything
      even the tiles in the men's room at the
Union Station will be
true

   all those mirrors there
   finally with faces in them

                  roses
              forests
          no more policemen
        no more
me.

for the mercy-mongers

it is justified
all dying is justified
all killing all death all
passing,
nothing is in vain
not even the neck
of a fly,

and a flower
passes through the armies
and like a small boy
bragging,
lifts up its
color.

IV

Burning In Water
Drowning In Flame

Poems 1972-1973

if you think I have gone crazy
try picking a flower from the garden of your
neighbor

now

I had boils the size of tomatoes
all over me
they stuck a drill into me
down at the county hospital,
and
just as the sun went down
everyday
there was a man in a nearby ward
he'd start hollering for his friend Joe.
JOE! he'd holler, OH JOE! JOE! J O E !
COME GET ME, JOE!

Joe never came by.
I've never heard such mournful
sounds.

Joe was probably working off a
piece of ass or
attempting to solve a crossword puzzle.

I've always said
if you want to find out who your friends are
go to a madhouse or
jail.

and if you want to find out where love is not
be a perpetual
loser.

I was very lucky with my boils
being drilled and tortured
against the backdrop of the Sierra Madre mountains
while that sun went down;
when that sun went down I knew what *I* would do
when I finally got that drill in my hands
like I have it
now.

the trash men

here they come
these guys
grey truck
radio playing

they are in a hurry

it's quite exciting:
shirt open
bellies hanging out

they run out the trash bins
roll them out to the fork lift
and then the truck grinds it upward
with far too much sound . . .

they had to fill out application forms
to get these jobs
they are paying for homes and
drive late model cars

they get drunk on Saturday night

now in the Los Angeles sunshine
they run back and forth with their trash bins

all that trash goes somewhere

and they shout to each other

then they are all up in the truck
driving west toward the sea

none of them know
that I am alive

REX DISPOSAL CO.

the elephants are caked with mud and tired
and the rhinos don't move
the zebras are stupid dead stems
and the lions don't roar
the lions don't care
the vultures are overfed
the crocodiles don't move
and there was a strange type of monkey,
I forget the name,
he was on a shelf up there, this male,
he topped the female and worked one off,
finished,
fell on his back and grinned,
and I said to my girlfriend,
let's go, at last something's happened.

back at my place we talked about it.

the zoo is a very sad place, I said,
taking my clothes off.

only those 2 monkeys seemed happy, she said,
getting out of her
clothes.

did you see that look on the male monkey's face?
I asked.

you look just like that afterwards, she
said.

later in the mirror I saw
a strange type of monkey. and
wondered about the giraffes and the
rhinos, and the elephants, especially the
elephants.

we'll have to go to the zoo
again.

I went to this place to see a movie
on tv
Alexander the Great,
and here come the armies
ta ta ta
horses, spears, knives, swords, shields,
men falling . . .
then turn to a roller derby —
here's a girl strangling another,
then back to Alexander —
a guy jumps out and assassinates Alex's father,
Alex kills the guy, Alex is king,
back to the roller derby — .
a man is down across the track and another man rams his head
with his skates —
and here come the armies
they appear to be fighting in a cave, there's smoke and
flame, swords,
men falling —
the Thunderbirds are behind,
one girl dives under another girl's ass,
throws her into the rail —
Alexander stands there listening to a guy who is holding
a glass of wine in his hand, and this boy is really telling
Alex wherehow, you know, and he turns his back to walk away
and Alex spears him —
the Thunderbirds are behind, they send out
Big John —
ta ta ta, here come the armies
they are splashing through water
through forests, they are going to get it
all
ta ta ta —
Big John didn't make it,
the girls are out again now —
Alexander is dying
Alexander the Great is dying
and they pass by his pallet in the open
he is dressed in fancy black garb and looks like
Richard Burton
the boys have their helmets off as they pass

and there's Alex's love by the pallet, and then
Alex begins to go, some men rush up,
one asks, Alex, who do you turn the rule over to?
who will rule now?
they wait.
he says, the strongest, and he dies
we are shown the clouds, the heavens,
way up there, and —
the Thunderbirds pull it out
in the last 12 seconds, they win it
112 to 110,
the crowd is consumed with Joy,
mercury bleeds into the light,
good night, sweet prince,
hail Mary,
Jesus Christ, what a
night.

lost

no

we can't we can't win it

I've decided we can't win it

just for a while we thought we could
but that was just for a while

now we know we can't win it

we can't stand still and win it
or run and win it

or do right and win it

or do wrong and win it

somebody else is going to win it

that's why somebody else is there and
we are here

it is terrible to be defeated
in what seems to count

it will happen

to accept it is impossible

to know it is more important
than doves or switchbrakes or
love.

hot

she was hot, she was so hot
I didn't want anybody else to have her,
and if I didn't get home on time
she'd be gone, and I couldn't bear that —
I'd go mad . . .
it was foolish I know, childish,
but I was caught in it, I was caught.

I delivered all the mail
and then Henderson put me on the night pickup run
in an old army truck,
the damn thing began to heat halfway through the run
and the night went on
me thinking about my hot Miriam
and jumping in and out of the truck
filling mailsacks
the engine continuing to heat up
the temperature needle was at the top
HOT   HOT
like Miriam.

I leaped in and out
3 more pickups and into the station
I'd be, my car
waiting to get me to Miriam who sat on my blue couch
with scotch on the rocks
crossing her legs and swinging her ankles
like she did,
2 more stops . . .
the truck stalled at a traffic light, it was hell
kicking it over
again . . .
I had to be home by 8, 8 was the deadline for Miriam.

I made the last pickup and the truck stalled at a signal
1/2 block from the station . . .
it wouldn't start, it couldn't start . . .
I locked the doors, pulled the key and ran down to the
station . . .
I threw the keys down. . . . signed out . . .
your god damned truck is stalled at the signal,

I shouted,
Pico and Western . . .

. . . I ran down the hall, put the key into the door,
opened it. . . . her drinking glass was there, and a note:

> *sun of a bitch:*
> *I wated until 5 after ate*
> *you don't love me*
> *you sun of a bitch*
> *somebody will love me*
> *I been wateing all day*
>
> *Miriam*

I poured a drink and let the water run into the tub
there were 5,000 bars in town
and I'd make 25 of them
looking for Miriam

her purple teddy bear held the note
as he leaned against a pillow

I gave the bear a drink, myself a drink
and got into the hot
water.

love

love, he said, gas
kiss me off
kiss my lips
kiss my hair
my fingers
my eyes my brain
make me forget

love, he said, gas
he had a room on the 3rd floor,
rejected by a dozen women
35 editors
and half a dozen hiring agencies,
now I'm not saying he was any
good

he turned on all the jets
without lighting them
and went to bed

some hours later a guy on his
way to room 309
lit a cigar in the
hall

and a sofa flew out the window
one wall shivered down like wet sand
a purple flame waved 40 feet high in the air

the guy in bed
didn't know or care
but I'd have to say
he was pretty good
that day.

burn and burn and burn

I used to know a dutchman in a Philly bar
he'd take 3 raw eggs in his beer,
71, still
working,
strong,
and there I sat down from him
4 or 5 barstools away
in my 20's
frightened
suicidal
unloved.
well, you know, sorrows beget
sorrows
burn and burn and burn and burn,
then something else takes
place.
I'm not saying it's as good
but it's certainly
more comfortable,
and often nights now
I think of that old dutchman —
I can look back on almost
a lifetime —

yet still remember him there
my master, then and
now.

the way

murdered in the alleys of the land
frost-bitten against flagpoles
pawned by females

educated in the dark for the dark

vomiting into plugged toilets
in rented rooms full of roaches and mice

no wonder we seldom sing
day or noon or night

the useless wars
the useless years
the useless loves

and they ask us,
why do you drink so much?

well, I suppose the days were made
to be wasted
the years and the loves were made
to be wasted.

we can't cry, and it helps to laugh —
it's like letting out
dreams, ideals,
poisons

don't ask us to sing,
laughing is singing to us,
you see, it was a terrible joke

Christ should have laughed on the cross,
it would have petrified his killers

now there are more killers than ever
and I write poems for them.

out of the arms . . .

out of the arms of one love
and into the arms of another

I have been saved from dying on the cross
by a lady who smokes pot
writes songs and stories,
and is much kinder than the last,
much much kinder,
and the sex is just as good or better.

it isn't pleasant to be put on the cross and left there,
it is much more pleasant to forget a love which didn't
work
as all love
finally
doesn't work . . .

it is much more pleasant to make love
along the shore in Del Mar
in room 42, and afterwards
sitting up in bed
drinking good wine, talking and touching
smoking

listening to the waves . . .

I have died too many times
believing and waiting, waiting
in a room
staring at a cracked ceiling
waiting for the phone, a letter, a knock, a sound . . .
going wild inside
while she danced with strangers in nightclubs . . .

out of the arms of one love
and into the arms of another

it's not pleasant to die on the cross,
it's much more pleasant to hear your name whispered in
the dark.

166

death of an idiot

he spoke to mice and sparrows
and his hair was white at the age of 16.
his father beat him every day and his mother
lit candles in the church.
his grandmother came while the boy slept
and prayed for the devil to let loose his hold upon
him
while his mother listened and cried over the
bible.

he didn't seem to notice young girls
he didn't seem to notice the games boys played
there wasn't much he seemed to notice
he just didn't seem interested.

he had a very lárge, ugly mouth and the teeth
stuck out
and his eyes were small and lusterless.
his shoulders were slumped and his back was bent
like an old man's.

he lived in our neighborhood.
we talked about him when we got bored and then
went on to more interesting things.
he seldom left his house. we would have liked to
torture him
but his father
who was a huge and terrible man
tortured him for
us.

one day the boy died. at 17 he was still a
boy. a death in a small neighborhood is noted with
alacrity, and then forgotten 3 or 4 days
later.

but the death of this boy seemed to stay with us
all. we kept talking about it
in our boy-men's voices
at 6 p.m. just before dark
just before dinner.

and whenever I drive through that neighborhood now
decades later
I still think of his death
while having forgotten all the other deaths
and everything else that happened
then.

tonalities

the soldiers march without guns
the graves are empty
peacocks glide in the rain

down stairways march great men smiling

there is food enough and rent enough and
time enough

our women will not grow old

I will not grow old

bums wear diamonds on their fingers

Hitler shakes hands with a Jew

the sky smells of roasted flesh

I am a burning curtain

I am steaming water

I am a snake I am an edge of glass that cuts
I am blood

I am this fiery snail
crawling home.

hey, dolly

she left me 5 weeks ago and went to Utah.
that is, I think she left.
the other day I went out to mail her a letter
and I saw her sitting on the bus stop bench,
it was her hair there
from behind
and all the pounding started in me again
I walked up quickly and looked at the face —
it was somebody else. freckles, pugnose, greeneyes,
nothing, nothing.

then I was on Western Avenue going from bar to bar
and I saw her in front of me again.
I saw those tight pants, I knew that ass,
and there was the hair again,
and the way she walked,
I walked faster to catch her,
I got even with her and saw her face —
an Indian's nose, blue eyes, a mouth like a frog —
nothing, nothing, nothing.

then there was a girl in a bar playing piano.
it wasn't her but when the hair fell in a certain way,
for a moment, it was. and the hair was the same length
and the lips were similar but not the same, and
she saw me looking while she was singing, I was drunk,
of course, it helped the delusion, and she
said, is there anything special you want to hear?
Dolly, I said, and she sang —

Hey, Dolly . . .

just now I looked up and she was across the street.
she walked out of the apartment across the street
with a young blond man and she stood there in sun glasses,
and I thought, what's she doing across the street in
sun glasses, and she smiled at me through the window
but she didn't wave and then she got in the car with the
young man, it was a new car, small and red, expensive,
and they drove away toward the west. I'm sure it was
her, this time.

a poorly night

you came out, she said,
and then you kicked this guy's car
and then you threw yourself into a bush
you crushed the whole
bush,
I don't know what your agony is all
about
but don't you think you should see a shrink?
I've got an awful good shrink, you'd
like him.

answer me, she said,
I get worried about the police when you
act like that, I'm very paranoid about the
police.

answer me, she said, why do you
act like that?

listen, she said, do you want me to
leave?

after she left I picked up a chair and
threw it out the window. there was much
glass and the screen was broken
too.

how many dead beasts float and walk from Wales to
Los Angeles?

looking for a job

it was Philly and the bartender said
what and I said, gimme a draft, Jim,
got to get the nerves straight, I'm
going to look for a job. you, he said,
a job?
yeah, Jim, I saw something in the paper,
no experience necessary.
and he said, hell, you don't want a job,
and I said, hell no, but I need money,
and I finished the beer
and got on the bus and I watched the numbers
and soon the numbers got closer
and then I was right there
and I pulled the cord and the bus stopped and
I got off.
it was a large building made of tin
the sliding door was stuck in the dirt
I pulled it back and went in
and there wasn't any floor, just more ground,
lumpy, wet, and it stank
and there were sounds like things being sawed in half
and things drilled and it was dark
and men walked on girders overhead
and men pushed trucks across the ground
and men sat at machines doing things
and there were shots of lightning and thunder
and suddenly a bucket full of flame came swinging at
my head, it roared and boiled with flame
it hung from a loose chain and it came right at me
and somebody hollered, HEY, LOOK OUT!
and I just ducked under the bucket
feeling the heat go over me,
and somebody asked,
WHAT DO YOU WANT?
and I said, WHERE IS YOUR NEAREST CRAPPER?
and I was told
and I went inside
then came out and saw silhouettes of men
moving through flame and sound and
I walked to the door, got outside, and
took the bus back to the bar and sat down

and ordered another draft, and Jim asked,
what happened? I said, they didn't want me, Jim.
then this whore came in and sat down and everybody
looked at her, she looked fine, and I remember it
was the first time in my life I almost wished I had a
vagina and clit instead of what I had, but in 2 or 3 days
I got over that and I was reading the
want ads again.

the 8 count

this one
always arrives at the wrong time

a basically good sort
I suppose
an honest man

but he doesn't take the 8 count
well

we're all beaten
but somehow
it's the manner in which he takes the count

after a visit from him
I am sickened for 3 or 4 days

I give him board and shelter and sometimes
money

but how he snarls and bitches
sucking at my cans of beer

if he expects deliverance in return for what he gives
he isn't going to get deliverance
because he doesn't give anything

no light
no love
no laughter no learning
nothing to
remember

the way of this one sickens me
he brings me sorrow when I have sorrow
he brings me madness when I have madness

I am a selfish man

over his last sweaty handshake
I told him I could carry him no longer

now when my soul has to puke
it will puke of its own
volition
and not from a
knock upon the
door.

dogfight

he's a runt
he snarls and scratches
chases cars
groans in his sleep
and has a perfect star above each eyebrow

we hear it outside:
he's ripping the shit out of something out there
5 times his
size

it's the professor's dog from across the street
that educated expensive bluebook dog
o, we're all in trouble

I pull them apart
and we run inside with the runt
bolt the door
flick out the lights
and see them crossing the street
immaculate and concerned

it looks like 7 or 8 people
coming to get their
dog

that big bag of jelly with hair
he ought to know better than to cross
the railroad tracks.

letters

she sits on the floor
going through a cardboard box
reading me love letters I have written her
while her 4 year old daughter lies on the floor
wrapped in a pink blanket and
three-quarters asleep

we have gotten together after a split
I sit in her house on a
Sunday night

the cars go up and down the hill outside
when we sleep together tonight
we will hear the crickets

where are the fools who don't live as
well as I?

I love her walls
I love her children
I love her dog

we will listen to the crickets
my arm curled about her hip
my fingers against her belly

one night like this beats life,
the overflow takes care of death

I like my love letters
they are true

ah, she has such a beautiful ass!
ah, she has such a beautiful soul!

yes yes

when God created love He didn't help most
when God created dogs He didn't help dogs
when God created plants that was average
when God created hate we had a standard utility
when God created me He created me
when God created the monkey He was asleep
when He created the giraffe He was drunk
when He created narcotics He was high
and when He created suicide He was low

when He created you lying in bed
He knew what He was doing
He was drunk and He was high
and He created the mountains and the sea and fire
at the same time

He made some mistakes
but when He created you lying in bed
He came all over His Blessed Universe.

eddie and eve

you know
I sat on the same barstool in Philadelphia for
5 years

I drank canned heat and the cheapest wine
I was beaten in alleys by well-fed truck drivers
for the amusement of the
ladies and gentlemen of the night

I won't tell you of my life as a child
it's too sickening
unreal

but what I mean
I finally went to see my friend Eddie
after 30 years

he was still in the same house
with the same wife

you guessed it:
he looked worse than I did

he couldn't get out of his chair

a cane
arthritis

what hair he had was
white

my god, Eddie, I said.

I know, he said, I've had it, I
can't breathe.

then his wife came out. the once slim
Eve I used to flirt with.

210 pounds
squinting at me.

my god, Eve, I said.
I know, she said.

we got drunk together. it was several hours later
Eddie said to me,
take her to bed, do her some good,
I can't do her any good any
more.

Eve giggled.

I can't Eddie, I said, you're my
buddy.

we drank some more.
endless quarts of
beer.

Eddie began to vomit.
Eve brought him a dishpan
and he vomited into the
dishpan
telling me between spasms
that we were men
real men
we knew what it was all about
by god
these young punks
didn't have it.

we carried him to bed
undressed him
and he was soon out,
snoring.

I said goodbye to Eve.
I got out and got into my car
and sat there staring at the house.
then I drove off.
it was all I had left to do.

the fisherman

he comes out at 7:30 a.m. every day
with 3 peanut butter sandwiches, and
there's one can of beer
which he floats in the baitbucket.
he fishes for hours with a small trout pole
three-quarters of the way down the pier.
he's 75 years old and the sun doesn't tan him,
and no matter how hot it gets
the brown and green lumberjack stays on.
he catches starfish, baby sharks, and mackerel;
he catches them by the dozen,
speaks to nobody.
sometime during the day
he drinks his can of beer.
at 6 p.m. he gathers his gear and his catch
walks down the pier
across several streets
where he enters a small Santa Monica apartment
goes to the bedroom and opens the evening paper
as his wife throws the starfish, the sharks, the mackerel
into the garbage

he lights his pipe
and waits for dinner.

warm asses

this Friday night
the Mexican girls at the Catholic carnival
look especially good
their husbands are in the bars
and the Mexican girls look young
hawk-nosed with cruel strong eyes,
asses warm in tight bluejeans
they have been taken somehow,
their husbands are tired of those warm asses
and the young Mexican girls walk with their children,
there is real sorrow in their cruel strong eyes,
as they remember nights when their handsome men —
not now any longer handsome —
said such beautiful things to them
beautiful things they will never hear again,
and under the moon and in the flashing of the
carnival lights
I see it all and I stand quietly and mourn for them.
they see me looking —
the old goat is looking at us
he's looking at our eyes;
they smile at each other, talk, walk off together,
laugh, look at me over their shoulders.
I walk over to a booth
put a dime on number eleven and win a chocolate cake
with 13 colored suckers stuck in the
top.
that's fair enough for an ex-Catholic
and an admirer of warm and young and
no-longer used
mournful Mexican asses.

what's the use of a title?

they don't make it
the beautiful die in flame —
suicide pills, rat poison, rope, what-
ever . . .
they rip their arms off,
throw themselves out of windows,
they pull their eyes from the sockets,
reject love
reject hate
reject, reject.

they don't make it
the beautiful can't endure,
they are the butterflies
they are the doves
they are the sparrows,
they don't make it.

one tall shot of flame
while the old men play checkers in the park
one flame, one good flame
while the old men play checkers in the park
in the sun.

the beautiful are found at the edge of a room
crumpled into spiders and needles and silence
and we can never understand why they
left, they were so
beautiful.

they don't make it,
the beautiful die young
and leave the ugly to their ugly lives.

lovely and brilliant: life and suicide and death
as the old men play checkers in the sun
in the park.

the tigress

terrible arguments.
and, at last, lying peacefully
on her large bed
which is
spread in red with cool patterns of flowers,
my head and belly down
head sideways
sprayed by shaded light
as she bathes quietly in the
other room,
it is all beyond me,
as most things are,
I listen to classical music on the small radio,
she bathes, I hear the splashing of water.

the catch

crud, he said,
hauling it out of the water,
what is it?

a Hollow-Back June Whale, I said.

no, said a guy standing by us on the pier,
it's a Billow-Wind Sand-Groper.

a guy walking by said,
it's a Fandango Escadrille without stripes.

we took the hook out and the thing stood up and
farted. it was grey and covered with hair
and fat and it stank like old socks.

it began to walk down the pier and we followed it.
it ate a hot dog and bun right out of the hands of
a little girl. then it leaped on the merry-go-round
and rode a pinto. it fell off near the end and
rolled in the sawdust.

we picked it up.

grop, it said, grop.

then it walked back out on the pier.
a large crowd followed us as we walked along.

it's a publicity stunt, said somebody,
it's a man in a rubber suit.

then as it was walking along it began to breathe
very heavily. it fell on its
back and began to thrash.

somebody poured a cup of beer over its head.

grop, it went, grop.

then it was dead.

we rolled it to the edge of the pier and pushed it
back into the water. we watched it sink and vanish.

it was a Hollow-Back June Whale, I said.

no, said the other guy, it was a Billow-Wind Sand-Groper.

no, said the other expert, it was a Fandango Escadrille
without stripes.

then we all went our way on a mid-afternoon in August.

wax job

man, he said, sitting on the steps
your car sure needs a wash and wax job
I can do it for you for 5 bucks,
I got the wax, I got the rags, I got everything
I need.

I gave him the 5 and went upstairs.
when I came down 4 hours later
he was sitting on the steps drunk
and offered me a can of beer.
he said he'd get the car the next
day.

the next day he got drunk again and
I loaned him a dollar for a bottle of
wine. his name was Mike
a world war II veteran.
his wife worked as a nurse.

the next day I came down and he was sitting
on the steps and he said,
you know, I been sitting here looking at your car,
wondering just how I was gonna do it,
I wanna do it real good.

the next day Mike said it looked like rain
and it sure as hell wouldn't make any sense
to wash and wax a car when it was gonna rain.

the next day it looked like rain again.
and the next.
then I didn't see him anymore.
a week later I saw his wife and she said,
they took Mike to the hospital,
he's all swelled-up, they say it's from the
drinking.

listen, I told her, he said he was going to wax my
car, I gave him 5 dollars to wax my
car.

he's in the critical ward, she said,
he might die . . .

I was sitting in their kitchen
drinking with his wife
when the phone rang.
she handed the phone to me.
it was Mike. listen, he said, come on down and
get me, I can't stand this
place.

I drove on down there, walked into the
hospital, walked up to his bed and
said, let's go Mike.

they wouldn't give him his clothes
so Mike walked to the elevator in his
gown.

we got on and there was a kid driving the
elevator and eating a popsicle.
nobody's allowed to leave here in a gown,
he said.

you just drive this thing, kid, I said,
we'll worry about the gown.

Mike was all puffed-up, triple size
but I got him into the car somehow
and gave him a cigarette.

I stopped at the liquor store for 2 six packs
then went on in. I drank with Mike and his wife until
11 p.m.
then went upstairs . . .

where's Mike? I asked his wife 3 days later,
you know he said he was going to wax my car.

Mike died, she said, he's gone.

you mean he died? I asked.

yes, he died, she said.

I'm sorry, I said, I'm very sorry

it rained for a week after that and I figured the only
way I'd get the 5 back was to go to bed with his wife
but you know
she moved out 2 weeks later

an old guy with white hair moved in there
and he had one blind eye and played the French Horn.
there was no way I could make it with
him.

some people

some people never go crazy.
me, sometimes I'll lie down behind the couch
for 3 or 4 days.
they'll find me there.
it's Cherub, they'll say, and
they pour wine down my throat
rub my chest
sprinkle me with oils.

then, I'll rise with a roar,
rant, rage —
curse them and the universe
as I send them scattering over the
lawn.
I'll feel much better,
sit down to toast and eggs,
hum a little tune,
suddenly become as lovable as a
pink
overfed whale.

some people never go crazy.
what truly horrible lives
they must lead.

father, who art in heaven —

my father was a practical man.
he had an idea.
you see, my son, he said,
I can pay for this house in my lifetime,
then it's mine.
when I die I pass it on to you.
now in your lifetime you can acquire a house
and then you'll have two houses
and you'll pass those two houses on to your
son, and in his lifetime he acquires a house,
then when he dies, his son —

I get it, I said.

my father died while trying to drink a
glass of water. I buried him.
solid mahogany casket. after the funeral
I went to the racetrack, met a high yellow.
after the races we went to her apartment
for dinner and goodies.

I sold his house after about a month.
I sold his car and his furniture
and gave away all his paintings except one
and all his fruit jars
(filled with fruit boiled in the heat of summer)
and put his dog in the pound.
I dated his girlfriend twice
but getting nowhere
I gave it up.

I gambled and drank away the money.

now I live in a cheap front court in Hollywood
and take out the garbage to
hold down the rent.

my father was a practical man.
he choked on that glass of water
and saved on hospital
bills.

nerves

twitching in the sheets —
to face the sunlight again,
that's clearly
trouble.
I like the city better when the
neon lights are going and
the nudies dance on top of the
bar
to the mauling music.

I'm under this sheet
thinking.
my nerves are hampered by
history —
the most memorable concern of mankind
is the guts it takes to
face the sunlight again.

love begins at the meeting of two
strangers. love for the world is
impossible. I'd rather stay in bed
and sleep.

dizzied by the days and the streets and the years
I pull the sheets to my neck.
I turn my ass to the wall.
I hate the mornings more than
any man.

the rent's high too

there are beasts in the salt shaker
and airdromes in the coffeepot.
my mother's hand is in the bag drawer
and from the backs of spoons come
the cries of tiny tortured animals.

in the closet stands a murdered man
wearing a new green necktie
and under the floor,
there's a suffocating angel with flaring nostrils.

it's hard to live here.
it's very hard to live here.

at night the shadows are unborn creatures.
beneath the bed
spiders kill tiny white ideas.

the nights are bad
the nights are very bad
I drink myself to sleep
I have to drink myself to sleep.

in the morning
over breakfast
I see them roll the dead down the street
(I never read about this in the newspapers).

and there are eagles everywhere
sitting on the roof, on the lawn, inside my car.
the eagles are eyeless and smell of sulphur.
it is very discouraging.

people visit me
sit in chairs across from me
and I see them crawling with vermin —
green and gold and yellow bugs
they do not brush away.

I have been living here too long.
soon I must go to Omaha.

they say that everything is jade there
and does not move.
they say you can stitch designs in the water
and sleep high in olive trees.
I wonder if this is
true?

I can't live here much longer.

laugh literary

listen, man, don't tell me about the poems you
sent, we didn't receive them,
we are very careful with manuscripts
we bake them
burn them
laugh at them
vomit on them
pour beer over them
but generally we return
them
they are
so
inane.
ah, we believe in Art,
we need it
surely,
but, you know, there are many people
(most people)
playing and fornicating with the
Arts
who only crowd the stage
with their generous unforgiving
vigorous
mediocrity.

our subscription rates are $4 a year.
please read our magazine before
submitting.

deathbed blues

if you can't stand the heat, he says, get out of the
kitchen. you know who said that?
Harry Truman.

I'm not in the kitchen, I say, I'm in the
oven.

my editor is a difficult man.
I sometimes phone him in moments of doubt.

look, he answers, you'll be lighting cigars with ten dollar
bills, you'll have a redhead on one arm and a blonde
on the other.

other times he'll say, look, I think I'm going to hire
V.K. as my associate editor. we've got to prune off
5 poets here somewhere. I'm going to leave it up
to him. (V.K. is a very imaginative poet who believes I've
knifed him from N.Y.C. to the shores of Hawaii.)

look, kid, I phone my editor, can you speak German?
no, he says.
well, anyhow, I say, I need some good new tires, cheap.
so you know where I can get some good new tires, cheap?
I'll phone you in 30 minutes, he says, will you be in
in 30 minutes?
I can't afford to go anywhere, I say.
he says, they say you were drunk at that reading
in Oregon.
ugly gossips, I answer.

were you?

I don't
remember.

one day he phones me:
you're not hitting the ball anymore. you *are* hitting the
bottle and fighting with all these
women. you know we got a good kid on the bench,
he's aching to get in there

he hits from both sides of the plate
he can catch anything that ain't hit over the wall
he's coached by Duncan, Creeley, Wakoski
and he can *rhyme*, he knows
images, similes, metaphors, figures, conceits,
assonance, alliteration, metrics, yes
metrics like, you know —
iambic, trochaic, anapestic, spondaic,
he knows caesura, denotation, connotation, personification,
diction, voice, paradox, rhetoric, tone *and*
coalescence . . .

holy shit, I say, hang up and take a good hit of
Old Grandad. Harry's still alive
according to the papers. but I decide rather than
getting new tires to get
a set of retreads instead.

charles

92 years old
his tooth has been bothering him
had to get it filled

he lost his left eye 40 years
ago

— a butcher, he says, he just wanted to
operate to get the money. I found out
later it coulda been
saved.

— I take the eye out at night, he says,
it hurts. they never did get it right.

— which eye is it, Charles?

— this one here, he points,
then excuses himself. he has to get up and
go into the
kitchen. he's baking cookies in the oven.

he comes out soon with a
plate.

— try some.

I do. they're
good.

— want some coffee? he asks.

— no, thanks, Charles, I haven't been sleeping
nights.

he got married at 70 to a woman
58. 22 years ago. she's in a rest home now.

— she's getting better, he says, she recognizes me.
they let her get up to go to the bathroom.

— that's fine, Charles.

— I can't stand her damned daughter, though, they think
I'm after her money.

— is there anything I can do for you, Charles? need
anything from the store, anything like
that?

— no, I just went shopping this morning.

his back is as straight as the wall and he has the
tiniest pot
belly. as he talks he
keeps his one eye on the tv set.

— I'm going now, Charles, you got my phone number?

— yeh.

— how are the girls treating you, Charles?

— my friend, I haven't thought about girls for some
years now.

— goodnight, Charles.

— goodnight.

I go to the door
open it
close it

outside
the smell of freshly-baked cookies
follows me.

on the circuit

it was up in San Francisco
after my poetry reading.
it had been a nice crowd
I had gotten my money
I had this place upstairs
there was some drinking
and this guy started beating up on a fag
I tried to stop him
and the guy broke a window
deliberately.
I told them all to
get out
and she started hollering down to the guy
who had beat on the fag
and he kept calling her name back up
and then I remembered she had vanished for an hour
before the reading.
she did those things.
maybe not bad things
but consistently careless things
and I told her we were through
and to get out
and I went to bed
then hours later she walked in
and I said, what the hell are you doing here?
she was all wild, hair down in her face,
you're too callous, I said, I don't want you.
it was dark and she leaped at me:
I'll kill you, I'll kill you!
I was still too drunk to defend myself
and she had me down on the kitchen floor
and she clawed my face and
bit a hole in my arm.

then I went back to bed and listened to her heels
going down the hill.

my friend, andre

this kid used to teach at Kansas U.
then they moved him out
he went to a bean factory
then he and his wife moved to the coast
she got a job and worked while
he looked for a job as an actor.
I really want to be an actor, he told me,
that's all I want to be.
he came by with his wife.
he came by alone.
the streets around here are full of guys who
want to be actors.
I saw him yesterday.
he was rolling cigarettes.
I poured him some white wine.
my wife is getting tired of waiting, he said,
I'm going to teach karate.
his hands were swollen from hitting
bricks and walls and doors.
he told me about some of the great oriental
fighters. there was one guy so good
he could turn his head 180 degrees
to see who was behind him. that's very hard to do,
he said.
further: it's more difficult to fight 4 men properly placed
than to fight many more. when you have many more
they get in each other's way, and a good fighter who has
strength and agility can do well.
some of the great fighters, he said,
even suck their balls up into their bodies.
this can be done — to some extent — because there are
natural cavities in the body. . . . if you stand upsidedown
you will notice this.

I gave him a little more white wine,
then he left.
you know, sometimes making it with a typewriter
isn't so painful
after all.

i was glad

I was glad I had money in the Savings and Loan
Friday afternoon hungover
I didn't have a job

I was glad I had money in the Savings and Loan
I didn't know how to play a guitar
Friday afternoon hungover

Friday afternoon hungover
across the street from Norm's
across the street from The Red Fez

I was glad I had money in the Savings and Loan
split with my girlfriend and blue and demented
I was glad to have my passbook and stand in line

I watched the buses run up Vermont
I was too crazy to get a job as a driver of buses
and I didn't even look at the young girls

I got dizzy standing in line but I
just kept thinking I have money in this building
Friday afternoon hungover

I didn't know how to play the piano
or even hustle a damnfool job in a carwash
I was glad I had money in the Savings and Loan

finally I was at the window
it was my Japanese girl
she smiled at me as if I were some amazing god

back again, eh? she said and laughed
as I showed her my withdrawal slip and my passbook
as the buses ran up and down Vermont

the camels trotted across the Sahara
she gave me the money and I took the money
Friday afternoon hungover

I walked into the market and got a cart

and I threw sausages and eggs and bacon and bread in there
I threw beer and salami and relish and pickles and mustard in there

I looked at the young housewives wiggling casually
I threw t-bone steaks and porterhouse and cube steaks in my cart
and tomatoes and cucumbers and oranges in my cart

Friday afternoon hungover
split with my girlfriend and blue and demented
I was glad I had money in the Savings and Loan.

trouble with spain

I got in the shower
and burned my balls
last Wednesday.

met this painter called Spain,
no, he was a cartoonist,
well, I met him at a party
and everybody got mad at me
because I didn't know who he was
or what he did.

he was rather a handsome guy
and I guess he was jealous because
I was so ugly.
they told me his name
and he was leaning against the wall
looking handsome, and I said:
hey, Spain, I like that name: Spain.
but I don't like you. why don't we step out
in the garden and I'll kick the shit out of your
ass?

this made the hostess angry
and she walked over and rubbed his pecker
while I went to the crapper
and heaved.

but everybody's angry at me.
Bukowski, he can't write, he's had it.
washed-up. look at him drink.
he never used to come to parties.
now he comes to parties and drinks everything
up and insults real talent.
I used to admire him when he cut his wrists
and when he tried to kill himself with
gas. look at him now leering at that 19 year old
girl, and you know he
can't get it up.

I not only burnt my balls in that shower
last Wednesday, I spun around to get out of the burning

water and burnt my bunghole
too.

the rag.
she sat there, glooming.
I couldn't do anything with her.
it was raining.
she got up and left.
well, hell, here it is again, I thought
I picked up my drink and turned the radio up,
took the lampshade off the lamp
and smoked a cheap black bitter cigar
imported from Germany.
there was a knock on the door
and I opened the door
a little man stood in the rain
and he said,
have you seen a pigeon on your porch?
I told him I hadn't seen a pigeon on my porch
and he said if I saw a pigeon on my porch
to let him know.
I closed the door
sat down
and then a black cat leaped through the
window and jumped on my
lap and purred, it was a beautiful animal
and I took it into the kitchen and we both ate a
slice of ham.
then I turned off all the lights
and went to bed
and that black cat went to bed with me
and it purred
and I thought, well, somebody likes me,
then the cat started pissing,
it pissed all over me and all over the sheets,
the piss rolled across my belly and slid down my sides
and I said: hey, what's wrong with you?
I picked up the cat and walked him to the door
and threw him out into the rain
and I thought, that's very strange, that cat
pissing on me
his piss was cold as the rain.
then I phoned her
and I said, look, what's wrong with you? have you lost

your god damned mind?
I hung up and pulled the sheets off the bed
and got in and lay there listening to the rain.
sometimes a man doesn't know what to do about things
and sometimes it's best to lie very still
and try not to think at all
about anything.

that cat belonged to somebody
it had a flea collar.
I don't know about the
woman.

we, the artists —

in San Francisco the landlady, 80, helped me drag the green
Victrola up the stairway and I played Beethoven's 5th
until they beat on the walls.
there was a large bucket in the center of the room
filled with beer and winebottles;
so, it might have been the d.t.'s, one afternoon
I heard a sound something like a bell
only the bell was humming instead of ringing,
and then a golden light appeared in the corner of the room
up near the ceiling
and through the sound and light
shone the face of a woman, worn but beautiful,
and she looked down at me
and then a man's face appeared by hers,
the light became stronger and the man said:
we, the artists, are proud of you!
then the woman said: the poor boy is frightened,
and I was, and then it went away.
I got up, dressed, and went to the bar
wondering who the artists were and why they should be
proud of me. there were some live ones in the bar
and I got some free drinks, set my pants on fire with the
ashes from my corncob pipe, broke a glass deliberately,
was not rousted, met a man who claimed he was William
Saroyan, and we drank until a woman came in and
pulled him out by the ear and I thought, no, that can't be
William, and another guy came in and said: man, you talk
tough, well, listen, I just got out for assault and
battery, so don't mess with me! we went outside the
bar, he was a good boy, he knew how to duke, and it went
along fairly even, then they stopped it and we went
back in and drank another couple of hours. I walked
back up to my place, put on Beethoven's 5th and
when they beat on the walls I beat
back.

I keep thinking of myself young, then, the way I was,
and I can hardly believe it but I don't mind it.
I hope the artists are still proud of me
but they never came back
again.

the war came running in and next I knew
I was in New Orleans
walking into a bar drunk
after falling down in the mud on a rainy night.
I saw one man stab another and I walked over and
put a nickle in the juke box.
it was a beginning. San
Francisco and New Orleans were two of my
favorite towns.

i can't stay in the same
room with that woman for five minutes

I went over the other day
to pick up my daughter.
her mother came out with workman's
overalls on.
I gave her the child support money
and she laid a sheaf of poems on me by one
Manfred Anderson.
I read them.
he's great, she said.
does he send this shit out? I asked.
oh no, she said, Manfred wouldn't do that.
why?
well, I don't know exactly.
listen, I said, you know all the poets who
don't send their shit out.
the magazines aren't ready for them, she said,
they're too far advanced for publication.
oh for christ's sake, I said, do you really
believe that?
yes, yes, I really believe that, she
answered.
look, I said, you don't even have the kid ready
yet. she doesn't have her shoes on. can't you
put her shoes on?
your daughter is 8 years old, she said,
she can put her own shoes on.
listen, I said to my daughter, for christ's sake
will you put your shoes on?
Manfred never screams, said her mother.
OH HOLY JESUS CHRIST! I yelled
you see, you see? she said, you haven't changed.
what time is it? I asked.
4:30. Manfred did submit some poems once, she said,
but they sent them back and he was *terribly*
upset.
you've got your shoes on, I said to my daughter,
let's go.
her mother walked to the door with us.
have a nice day, she said.
fuck off, I said.

when she closed the door there was a sign pasted to
the outside. it said:
SMILE.
I didn't.
we drove down Pico on the way in.
I stopped outside the Red Ox.
I'll be right back, I told my daughter.
I walked in, sat down, and ordered a scotch and
water. over the bar there was a little guy popping in and
out of a door holding a very red, curved penis
in his hand.
can't
can't you make him stop? I asked the barkeep.
can't you shut that thing off?
what's the matter with you, buddy? he asked.
I submit my poems to the magazines, I said.
you submit your poems to the magazines? he asked.
you are god damned right I do, I said.
I finished my drink and got back to the car.
I drove down Pico Boulevard.
the remainder of the day was bound to be better.

charisma

this woman keeps phoning me
even though I tell her I am living with a woman
I love.

I keep hearing noises in the environment,
she phones,
I thought it was you.

me? I haven't been drunk for several
days.

well, maybe it wasn't you but I felt it was
somebody who was trying to help
me.

maybe it was God. do you think He's there?

yes, He's a hook from the ceiling.

I thought so.

I'm growing tomatoes in my basement,
she says.

that's sensible.

I want to move. where shall I move?

north is obvious. west is the ocean. the east is the
past. south is the only way.

south?

yes, but not past the border. it's death to
gringos.

what's Salinas like? she asks.

if you like lettuce
go to Salinas.

suddenly she hangs up. she always does that. and she
always phones back in a day or a week or a
month. she'll be at my funeral with tomatoes and the
yellow pages of the phonebook stuck into the pockets of
her mince-brown overcoat in 97 degree heat,
I have a way with the ladies.

the sound of human lives

strange warmth, hot and cold females,
I make good love, but love isn't just
sex. most females I've known are
ambitious, and I like to lie around
on large comfortable pillows at 3 o'clock
in the afternoon, I like to watch the sun
through the leaves of a bush outside
while the world out there
holds away from me, I know it so well, all
those dirty pages, and I like to lie around
my belly up to the ceiling after making love
everything flowing in:
it's so easy to be easy — if you let it, that's all
that's necessary.
but the female is strange, she is very
ambitious — shit! I can't sleep away the day!
all we do is eat! make love! sleep! eat! make love!

my dear, I say, there are men out there now
picking tomatoes, lettuce, even cotton,
there are men and women dying under the sun,
there are men and women dying in factories
for nothing, a pittance . . .
I can hear the sound of human lives being ripped to
pieces . . .
you don't know how lucky we
are . . .

but you've got it made, she says,
your poems . . .

my love gets out of bed.
I hear her in the other room.
the typewriter is working.

I don't know why people think effort and energy
have anything to do with
creation.

I suppose that in matters like politics, medicine,
history and religion

they are mistaken
also.

I turn on my belly and fall asleep with my
ass to the ceiling for a change.

you shoulda been at this party,
I know you hate parties
but you seem to be at most of them.
anyhow, I took my girl, you know
her —

Java Jane?

yes, this party was at the merry-go-round
where they are trying to tear the pier down, you
know where that is?

yes, the red paint, the broken
windows —

yes, anyhow, my girl lives in a room just above the
merry-go-round. it's a
birthday party for the woman who owns the
merrry-go-round.
she's trying to save the pier
she's trying to save the merry-go-round —
plenty of drinks for everybody, my girl lives in the
room right above the
merry-go-round.

sounds great.

I phoned. you weren't
in.

it's all right.

well, there was plenty to drink and they turned the
merry-go-round on, it was free, music and
everything.

sounds great.

my girlfriend and I got into an
argument, all the drinking —

of course.

I'm standing apart from her
she's standing apart from me.
she's got a glass of wine in her hand.
I give her a dark green deathly stare,
she's stricken
she steps back
the thing is whirling
a horse's hoof kicks her in the ass.
she drops down upon the spinning.
it all happens so fast —
but I do notice
that all the time she's circling
to the music under those horses
she's holding her glass upright
in order not to spill a
drop.

brave.

sure. only all the time her panties are
showing. glowing and glistening.
pink.

wonderful. how do they do it?

they conspire.

the glistening pink?

yes. so her panties are showing and I think
well, that's all right but it probably looks
a hell of a lot better to them than it does to
me, so I moved a step forward and said,
Jane.

what happened?

she kept spinning around holding her drink up
showing her pink bottom . . . there seemed something

tenuous about it, deliciously inane . . .

stunted glory finally comes forth hollering . . .

exactly. she kept gliding around
legs outspread —
dizzied with life —
vengeful —
she must have cared for me to show her
panties to all those
people. anyhow, she kept sliding around
until her leg hit one of this guy's legs —
he'd stepped forward for a closer look.
he was 67 years old and with his wife
and they were both
eating spaghetti off paper plates, anyhow,
my girl's leg hit his
she came bouncing off on her ass
still holding the glass of wine upright.
I walked over and picked her up
and she still held it
level, then she lifted it and
drank it.

sounds like it was a
fine party.

I phoned. you weren't
in.

spiderwebs of dripping
wet-dew sex like
badbreath dreams.

exactly. you should have been
there.

sorry.

burned

the kid went back to New York City to live with a woman
he met in a kibbutz.
he left his mother at the age of
32, a well-kept fellow, sense of humor and never
wore the same pair of shorts
more than one day. there he was
in the Puerto Rican section, she had a
job. he wanted iron bars on the windows and
ate too much fried chicken at 10 a.m.
in the morning after she went to
work. he had some money saved out of the
years and he fucked but he was really
afraid of
pussy.

I was sitting with Eileen in Hollywood
and I said:
I ought to warn the kid
so that when she turns on him
he'll be
ready.

no, she said, let him be happy.

I let him be
happy.

now he's back living with his
mother, he weighs three hundred and ten pounds
and eats all the time
and laughs all the time
but you ought to see his
eyes . . .
the eyes are sitting in the center of all that
flesh . . .

he bites into a chicken leg:
I loved her, he says to me,
I loved her.

hell hath no fury . . .

she was in her orange Volks waiting
as I walked up the street
with 2 six packs and a pint of scotch
and she jumped out
and began grabbing the beerbottles and
smashing them on the pavement
and she got the pint of scotch and
smashed that too,
saying: ho! so you were going to get her
drunk on this and fuck her!
I walked in the doorway where the other woman
stood halfway up the stairs,
then *she* ran in from the street
and up the stairs and hit the other woman
with her purse, saying:
he's my man! he's my man!
and then she ran out and
jumped into her orange Volks
and drove away.
I came out with a broom
and began sweeping up the glass
when I heard a sound
and there was the orange Volks
running on the sidewalk
and on me —
I managed to leap up against a wall
as it went by.
then I took the broom and began sweeping up
the glass again,
and suddenly she was standing there;
she took the broom and broke it into three
pieces,
then she found an unbroken beerbottle
and threw it at the glass window of the door.
it made a clean round hole
and the other woman shouted down from the
stairway: for God's sake, Bukowski, go with
her!

I got into the orange Volks and we
drove off together.

pull a string, a puppet moves . . .

each man must realize
that it can all disappear very
quickly:
the cat, the woman, the job,
the front tire,
the bed, the walls, the
room; all our necessities
including love,
rest on foundations of sand —
and any given cause,
no matter how unrelated:
the death of a boy in Hong Kong
or a blizzard in Omaha . . .
can serve as your undoing.
all your chinaware crashing to the
kitchen floor, your girl will enter
and you'll be standing, drunk,
in the center of it and she'll ask:
my god, what's the matter?
and you'll answer: I don't know,
I don't know . . .

tougher than corned beef hash —

the motion of the human heart:
strangled over Missouri;
sheathed in hot wax in Boston;
burned like a potato in Norfolk;
lost in the Allegheny Mountains;
found again in a 4-poster mahogany bed
in New Orleans;
drowned and stirred with pinto beans
in El Paso;
hung on a cross like a drunken dog
in Denver;
cut in half and toasted in
Kalamazoo;
found cancerous on a fishing boat
off the coast of Mexico;
tricked and caged at Daytona Beach;
kicked by a nursery maid
in a green and white ghingham dress,
waiting table at a North Carolina
bus stop;
rubbed in olive oil and goat-piss
by a chess-playing hooker in the East Village;
painted red, white, and blue
by an act of Congress;
torpedoed by a dyed blonde
with the biggest ass in Kansas;
gutted and gored by a woman
with the soul of a bull
in East Lansing;
petrified by a girl with tiny fingers,
she had one tooth missing,
upper front, and pumped gas
in Mesa;
the motion of the human heart goes on
and on
and on and on
for a while.

voices

1.

my moustache is pasted-on
and my wig and my eyebrows
and even my eyes . . .
then something stuns me . . .
the lampshades swing, I hear
simmering and magic and
incredible sounds.

2.

I know I went mad, almost as
an act of theory:
the lost are found
the sick are healthy
the non-creators are the
creators.

3.

even if I were a comfortable, domesticated
sophisticate I could never drink the
blood of the masses and
call it wine.

4.

why did I have to lift that pretty girl's
car by the bumper because the jack got stuck?
I couldn't straighten up
and they took me away like a pretzel and straightened
me but I still couldn't move . . .
it was the hospital's fault, the doctors' fault.
then those two boys dropped me on the way to the
x-ray room . . . I hollered LAWSUIT!
but I guess it was that girl's fault —

she shouldn't have shown me all that leg
and haunch.

5.

listen, listen, SPACESHIT LOVE, TORN IN DRIP OUT,
SPACESHIT LOVE, LOVE, LOVE; KILL, LEARN TO USE A
WEAPON; OPEN AREAS, REALIZE, BE DIVINE, SPACESHIT
LOVE, IT'S approaching . . .

6.

I did a take-off of E.H. in my first novel,
been living green ever since. I'm probably
the best journalist America ever had, I can
bullshit on any subject, and that counts for
something. you admire me much more
than the first man you meet on the street
in the morning. basically, though, it's a
fact, I've lived during an era of no writers
at all, so I've earned a position
because nothing else appeared. o.k.,
it's a bad age. I suppose I am number
one. But it's hardly the same as when we
had giants turning us on. forget it:
I'm living green.

7.

I was a bad writer, I killed N.C. because I made
more of him than there was, and then the *ins*
made more of my book than there was. there have
been only 3 bad writers in acceptable American
literature. Drieser, of course, was the worst.
then we had Thomas Wolfe, and then we had me. but
when I try to choose between me and Wolfe, I've
got to take Wolfe. I mean as the worst. I like
to think of what Capote, another bad writer said

about me: he just typewrites. sometimes even
bad writers tell the truth.

8.

my problem, like most, is artistic preciousness. I
exist, full of french fries and glory
and then I look around, see the Art-form, pop into
it and tell them how fine I am and what I think.
this is the same tiresomeness that has almost des-
troyed art for centuries. I made a record once of
myself reading my poems to a lion at the zoo. he really
roared, as if he were in pain. all the poets play
this record and laugh when they get drunk.

9.

remember my novel about jail where
photos of heroes and lovers floated against the
rock walls?
I got famous. I came over here.
I got hot for the black motorcyclists of Valley
West and Bakersfield
who took my fame and jammed it
and made me suck their loneliness and dementia
and their dream of Cadillac white soul and
Cadillac black soul
and they creamed up my ass
and into my nostrils and into my ears
while I said, Communism, Communism
and they grinned and knew I didn't mean it.

straight on through

I am
hung by a nail
the sun melts my heart
I am
cousin to the snake
and am afraid of waterfalls
I am
afraid of women and green walls

the police stop me and
tell me
while the trees whirl in the wind
(I am hungover) that my muffler is shot and
my windshield wiper doesn't work
and the lens on my back-up light is broken.
I don't have a back-up light,
sign the citation and am thankful,
inside,
that they don't take me in for what I'm
thinking

sadness drips like water beads
in a half-poisoned well,
I know that my chances have narrowed down to
almost nothing —
I'm like a bug in the bathroom when you flick on the
lightswitch at 3 a.m.

love, finally, with a washrag stuffed down its
throat, pictures of joy
turned to paperclips, you
know you know you know.
once you understand this process (what you
must understand
is
that most things
just won't work, so
you don't try to save

them, and by the time you learn this
you've run out of
years) — once you understand this process
you need only get burned 2 or 3 more times
before they stuff you away, and
it's good to know that —
stop being so fucking quick with your
rejoinders and relax —
you're about finished, too, just
like I am. no shame
there. I can walk into any bar and
order a scotch and water,
pay,
and put my hand around the glass,
they don't know, they won't know,
either about you or about me,
they'll talk about football and the
weather and the energy crisis,
and our hands will reach up
the mirror watching the hands
and we'll drink it down —

Jane, Barbara, Frances, Linda, Liza, Stella,
father's brown leather slipper
upsidedown in the bathroom,
nameless dead dogs,
tomorrow's newspaper,
water boiling out of the radiator on a
Thursday afternoon, burning your arm
halfway to the elbow, and not even being
angry at the pain,
grinning for the winners
grinning for the guy who fucked your girl
while you were drunk or away
and grinning for the girl who let him.
the roses howl
in the dim wind,
we have
said the necessary things, and
getting out is next, only I'd like

to say
no matter what they've said,
I've never been mad
at anything.

dreamlessly

old grey-haired waitresses
in cafes at night
have given it up,
and as I walk down sidewalks of
light and look into windows
of nursing homes
I can see that it is no longer
with them.
I see people sitting on park benches
and I can see by the way they
sit and look
that it is gone.

I see people driving cars
and I see by the way
they drive their cars
that they neither love nor are
loved —
nor do they consider
sex. it is all forgotten
like an old movie.

I see people in department stores and
supermarkets
walking down aisles
buying things
and I can see by the way their clothing
fits them and by the way they walk
and by their faces and their eyes
that they care for nothing
and that nothing cares
for them.

I can see a hundred people a day
who have given up
entirely.

if I go to a racetrack
or a sporting event
I can see thousands
that feel for nothing or

no one
and get no feeling
back.

everywhere I see those who
crave nothing but
food, shelter, and
clothing; they concentrate
on that,
dreamlessly.

I do not understand why these people do not
vanish
I do not understand why these people do not
expire
why the clouds
do not murder them
or why the dogs
do not murder them
or why the flowers and the children
do not murder them,
I do not understand.

I suppose they are murdered
yet I can't adjust to the
fact of them
because they are so
many.

each day,
each night,
there are more of them
in the subways and
in the buildings and
in the parks

they feel no terror
at not loving
or at not
being loved

so many many many
of my fellow
creatures.

palm leaves

at exactly 12:00 midnight
1973-74
Los Angeles
it began to rain on the
palm leaves outside my window
the horns and firecrackers
went off
and it thundered.

I'd gone to bed at 9 p.m.
turned out the lights
pulled up the covers —
their gaiety, their happiness,
their screams, their paper hats,
their automobiles, their women,
their amateur drunks . . .

New Year's Eve always terrifies
me

life knows nothing of years.

now the horns have stopped and
the firecrackers and the thunder . . .
it's all over in five minutes . . .
all I hear is the rain
on the palm leaves,
and I think,
I will never understand men,
but I have lived
it through.

Photo: Richard Robinson

CHARLES BUKOWSKI is one of America's best-known contemporary writers of poetry and prose, and, many would claim, its most influential and imitated poet. He was born in Andernach, Germany, to an American soldier father and a German mother in 1920, and brought to the United States at the age of three. He was raised in Los Angeles and lived there for fifty years. He published his first story in 1944 when he was twenty-four and began writing poetry at the age of thirty-five. He died in San Pedro, California, on March 9, 1994, at the age of seventy-three, shortly after completing his last novel, *Pulp* (1994).

During his lifetime he published more than forty-five books of poetry and prose, including the novels *Post Office* (1971), *Factotum* (1975), *Women* (1978), *Ham on Rye* (1982), and *Hollywood* (1989). Among his most recent books are the posthumous editions of *What Matters Most Is How Well You Walk Through the Fire* (1999), *Open All Night: New Poems* (2000), *Beerspit Night and Cursing: The Correspondence of Charles Bukowski and Sheri Martinelli, 1960-1967* (2001), and *Night Torn Mad with Footsteps: New Poems* (2001).

All of his books have now been published in translation in more than a dozen languages and his worldwide popularity remains undiminished. In the years to come Ecco will publish additional volumes of previously uncollected poetry and letters.